STOLEN

CLAIMED BY THE SEVEN REALMS - BOOK TWO

AIDY AWARD

Cover by Danielle Doolittle of Doelle Designs

For everyone who doesn't dance because they think they're too fat.
You're perfect the way you are.
Dance.
And fuck the haters.
(Well, not literally. That's a different kind of romance.
*wink)

To dance is to be out of yourself. Larger, more beautiful, more powerful... This is power, it is glory on Earth and it is yours for the taking.

— AGNES DEMILLE

STEEL IN THE WINTER REALM

CLARA

*I*n one breath I went from comfort and joy to death and despair. Honestly, that seemed pretty on pointe for life in the Winter Realm. One minute, I was filled with the magic of discovering this whole new world, falling in love, finding my mission in life, and getting the best orgasms from four of the hottest men to ever be born under the Christmas star, and the next someone was trying to kill is.

Yesterday felt about a million years away. I think time might move differently here in the realm than in the human world. Only a day had passed since Nuss dragged me through the portal between our worlds in our Stahlbaum family Christmas tree as we were chased by mice. But so much had happened since and I wouldn't trade even a second of it.

Well, maybe a couple of the seconds when I was being eaten alive by those horrid mice. But the rest? Good times, good times.

I gasped because, a horse jumped into our path from behind an outcropping of rocks, and my heart that had been flying sunk like a crashing Christmas bulb into the bottom of my stomach. There was one particular person in my life who liked to ruin anything I had that was even slightly nice. Of course, he would try to ruin this for me too.

"Hello, little sister." Fritz looked from my Viking, behind me on our horse, to Nuss, and back to Zucker and Tau. His mount side-stepped and jostled about as if it was uncomfortable, but my brother didn't seem bothered. "I always knew you were a whore."

He curled his lip the same way I'd seen him do when he had to help look after father. "You should have married Herr Drosselmeyer when you had the chance, if only to save the family's reputation."

Older brothers were the worst. Mine especially.

Here I was, excited about the adventures ahead of me, filled with love and magic, then Fritz had to come along and try to break my toys. A couple of days ago, his words would have burned into me and hurt. I may have only been in the Winter Realm a brief time, but this world, and the men I'd connected to in it, were more my family than Fritz ever was.

Family was what I was making here, not the blood bond Fritz and I shared. "What are you doing here, Friedrich?"

He hated when I called him that. It was an old Stahlbaum family name and he wanted to be more modern and sophisticated than that.

"I've been sent to bring you home. Cleaning up your little messes, just like always." Fritz flicked his hands over his pants, as if wiping away some kind of dirt. He was trying his best to appear like this conversation was boring and beneath him. That was always his super-power back home. Made everyone else around him feel little and stupid.

"You will watch your mouth when speaking to the princess." Leb's voice boomed, and I got more than a thrill from knowing he had my back, figuratively and literally.

Fritz's eyes snapped to evaluate Leb and I could practically see the calculations he was doing in his head to assess the threat. "You have no say in this, peasant. I am head of the Stahlbaum household and ClaraMarie is my responsibility."

Ooh. Someone who hadn't known what a scared little shit Fritz was, might have missed the way he sunk back in his saddle before he struck back. But I saw. With each jab in this battle of wits between us, my vision grew sharper, and my strategy whirred. Both were new sensations in my dealings with my brother. He knew he was outnumbered and out manned. This was a rare turn of the tables.

Welcome to my world, big brother.

Nuss looked to me, communicating with a simple look that I was in charge here. He waited until I nodded, then put himself between us and Fritz. "But we aren't in the human realm anymore, and any authority you thought you had over our Clara ended the moment you came through the Christmas tree portal."

Fritz's hand hovered over the scabbard at his side. When had he learned to ride or use a sword? He must not be greatly confident in his skills, because if he was, he would have drawn. It was unusual to see him unnerved. I was happy to take advantage of it.

The men were making it clear, I was the general in our army, and that gave me a rush just the same as when my magic had risen up last night.

I gave Nuss my thanks with a soft blink of my eyes, and he backed his horse up a few steps. There was something new inside of me and I was guessing it had something to do with my bond with Leb last night and the fact that he came from a race of warriors in a matriarchal society. With every move one of my men made, I felt more empowered, not less. That gave me the courage to call Fritz out on the real betrayal. "Not to mention that you joined the wrong side of this fight when you got cozy with the Mouse Queen."

The entire mountain went silent. I gave Fritz the

smiling smirk her deserved. "Didn't know I found out your dirty, little secret, did you?"

Leb snickered behind me, and I had to admit that having my guard around me gave me that extra bit of security I needed to stand my ground and even up the ante. I was a little surprised none of them had gone at him yet. I wasn't used to men both defending and deferring to me. It was something I could get used to though.

Fritz didn't like that I had the upper hand and that could go very badly if we weren't careful. While my brother was a dickhead and was in league with the wrong side, I also didn't want to see him killed.

"I'm not keeping any secrets, unlike you, little sister." His sneer was defensive this time. "I suggest you surrender and come with me quietly, so you don't cause any more trouble."

Tau and Zucker sidled up beside me and Leb, making a nice wall of muscle. I sat up even straighter. "You've got that backwards. You're the one who'll be coming with us so that you don't cause any more trouble. If you hadn't noticed, here in the Winter Realm, we're equals, and you're outnumbered."

The tingle of the magic I'd discovered inside of me last night, flowed along my skin. I swear, yesterday I didn't have this same confidence. There was more to how I was feeling and what was happening than I'd thought before. Bonding with Leb must have given me a little of his Viking spirit, because I was ready to take Fritz on head-to-head.

Learning some self-defense and even some offense was quickly rising up my priority list. I didn't want to get stuck throwing snowballs again and I sure would like to see Fritz flat on his back in the snow from a good swift kick to the knees. Or the family jewels. My magic went all zip and zing thinking about it, and Leb wrapped his hand around my waist, then leaned forward and whispered in my ear. "I can feel your magic rearing to get out and take this crumble of a man down. But save it, lass for the journey ahead. I'm more than happy to chop his head off for you."

Ooh. Why did Leb's bloodthirsty threat turn me on? "That sounds like fun, but alas I cannot condone killing my own kin, even if he is a royal ass. I'm having a bit of fun poking at him though. I don't normally get to in the human realm."

"Then have at. He needs a good blood-eagle to the soul." I could hear the contempt for Fritz in every one of Leb's words.

Now it was going to get fun. For me anyway. Not so much for Fritz. "Here's what going to happen, brother. You're going to ride down the mountain with us, and you're not going to say a word the whole way. When we get back to the Christmas tree for us you can either go home through the portal, and mind your own business, or you can come with us to the next land and maybe learn how you've chosen the wrong side."

Nuss drew his sword, Tau notched an arrow, Zucker twirled a dagger in his hand, and Leb laughed. It was the last that scared Fritz the most. He hated to be laughed at.

"You have no idea who I am here in your precious Winter Realm." He directed his ire at Leb, but I full-well knew that was a proxy for me.

I did wonder how long or how often he'd been here. Nuss implied the portal only opened to come here at midnight on Christmas morning, but that didn't explain how he'd gotten into the human realm before it opened. That was a question for later. "Doesn't matter, because I know who I am here."

I wasn't his doormat any longer. I had a mission to spread love, find those broken pieces of the seven crowns, and help my true people prepare to fight alongside the Vivandiere to defeat the Mouse Queen. Who apparently was Fritz's new special friend.

Gross.

Since he was my brother, I felt responsible for making sure he didn't make things worse here like he did at home. "We've got places to go, and I don't have time for your shenanigans. Fall in line. Now."

Ooh. I sounded so warrior woman.

"Now can I chop of his head with my axe, lass?" I felt Leb reaching for the axe on his back.

Fritz glared at me, dragging me into an old-fash-ioned stare down to see who would blink first. "I'm getting closer to saying yes."

"In the meantime, might I suggest we tie him up and make him walk?" Nuss nodded to Zucker and Tau and faster than I could say Christmas tree, the three of them had him surrounded, off his horse, hogtied, and gagged.

"Whoa." Seeing them so easily take Fritz down was exhilarating. "I was being a word warrior there for a minute, but you guys are like a coordinated troop of soldiers."

"Sweetheart," Zucker patted my thigh. "The warrior magic of the Gingerbread Kingdom was flowing through you straight to us. We were merely tapping into your power."

Fritz struggled and rolled around, but it did nothing but get him a face full of snow. Ha.

I turned in the saddle just enough to be able to see Leb better. "When we bonded, I thought we were awakening my magic, but you were giving me some of yours, weren't you?"

"I was in such a hurry to fuck you, we didn't even think about how little you know about how life in the realm works. But you've got the gist of it."

Fritz made some talking sounds that absolutely were slurs at me. I gave him the stink eye and Nuss stepped on his back, smashing him deeper into the snow. "This is part of why the four of us decided to stop competing against each other for who would be your consort."

"Only part?" I'd meant that to be a little joke

knowing that they were each as anxious as I was to find the other pieces of the crown that belong to their lands so we could consummate our bonds.

Nuss's eyes went dark, and I got the warm and fuzzies in my lower belly. That was the same look as when he was watching us from his throne in the corner of the room. It took me a really long minute to tear my eyes... and thoughts away.

Tau looked between us and grinned. "Yes, my flower, only part. But we did hope that combining what's in our souls with your magic would strengthen you, and thus all of the lands."

Zucker snickered. "Yeah, that's the part I was thinking about last night. Not the part where your--"

"Zzz. Pssst. Shh. That's enough of that kind of talk in front of my brother." I pretended to smooth my hair just to cover the way I knew my cheeks were lighting like bright red balloons. It wasn't that I was embarrassed or shameful about what we'd done. Just that it was meant to be between us.

And well, yes. I could do without Fritz's judgmental glares.

Zucker gave me a long, heated look and shoved Fritz's face deeper into the snow. "I'll hold my tongue now, if you'll hold it in your cunt later."

"Ahem. Yes, umm. Let's be on our way. Can we drop him off in the Christmas Tree Forest and shove him through the portal before our next destination?"

Nuss grabbed the back of Fritz's jacket and pulled

him up to his knees. "I think we'd better bring him back up the mountain to Mother Gingerbread. She'll get a good kick out of interrogating him, and we might learn how the Mouse Queen got to him."

"I'll never talk." Fritz spit snow from his mouth, sputtering at being manhandled. "Your mommy doesn't scare me."

Leb laughed that big hearty chuckle. "You should be ready to pee your pants, small boy. She scares the rest of us. But if you aren't that attached to your bollocks, feel free to tell her that yourself."

"I will." Fritz squirmed in Nuss's hold but didn't get anywhere.

"Let's bring him to the Land of Sweets. A good vat of boiling sugar poured over his cock should get him talking."

I looked at Tau and Nuss, both of whom shrugged. Tau shook his head. "My people can't do much more than whip him with some violets. Maybe the Snowflake nuns can guilt it out of him."

"Okay, Land of Sweets it is then." Nuss shoved Fritz toward his horse and tied him to the reins so that he'd have to walk behind.

Hmm. There was a story there and I wanted to hear it before we got to Nuss's land of Snowflakes. I hadn't even realized the Winter Realm had religion. I'm not sure why I assumed it didn't, really. Organized religion often came with the trappings of purity culture. That had to have something to do with why he didn't join in with us last night.

Could it be possible that my handsome and sexy Captain of the Nutcracker guard was a virgin?

"Come on now." Leb gave our horse a nudge with his feet. "Let's get a move on. It's already the second day of Christmas and we've got more crowns to find."

I had two already. The one from the Land of Spirit and Magic that my mother left me. Ha, take that Fritz. And the one from the Gingerbread Kingdom. But I only had three more princes to bond with.

But I'd kissed another.

WHERE IS THE VIVANDIERE?

CLARA

I glanced up along the path we'd come down and scowled. Nothing moved, yet something was out there. I don't know how I knew, but I felt the presence of the Dark Warrior, Konig, the Mouse Prince of the Land of Animals. Was he following us, watching? Had he watched us last night?

A messenger angel streaked down the mountain toward us and Nuss caught her on the elbow of his still broken arm. He flicked open the roll of paper and flashed us a warning look. "They've started their attack, Leb."

"Shite. Get that dickhead back on that horse and let's go. The mountain's defenses are set to trigger an avalanche. Let's go, go go." Leb snapped his reigns and took the lead down the rocky path.

"An avalanche? Sweet baby Jesus." I quickly checked that everyone was with us. I'd already been through losing them in the last battle. I didn't want to go through that again.

Nuss tossed Fritz up across the back of the horse like a trussed-up animal, and all three of them jumped onto their own rides. Leb gave us a hee-ya command and the six of us went barreling down the tiny path at a breakneck speed.

The mountain behind us rumbled and the spikes of anticipation already pumping from my heart screaming at me to run, went into flat out we're-all-going-to-die mode. A mountain of snow and rock and trees were in pursuit and catching us up fast.

"Nuss, we aren't going to make it. You got a plan?" Leb shouted, and I hoped someone had an idea. The snow was already flying around us and while Leb could probably survive an apocalypse, the rest of us were vulnerable.

"Fuck it. This was supposed to be a last resort." He pushed his horse to put on a burst of speed and rode up next to me. He kicked one leg over the horse, standing in one stirrup, hanging onto the reins with one arm like a fancy Lipizzaner rider doing tricks.

What the hell was he doing? Leb held me tight around the waist, as Nuss leaned in and going at lightning speed across jagged terrain with a fucking avalanche bearing down on us, he kissed me. Not just any kiss, either. Nuss sucked my bottom lip into his mouth and bit me.

I don't know how, but when he did that, he took some magic from me. The tingles of my newfound powers shimmered through my vision like snowflakes, over to Nuss. I yanked my mouth away and touched my lips. My fingers came away with a touch of blood.

Granted it would be hard to be gentle while galloping through an avalanche, but he'd done that on purpose. There had to be a reason. Nuss would never hurt me. What was going on?

He licked his own lips and then flipped backwards on his horse, pulled out his sword and aimed it at the snow.

What in the holy Christmas Star was going on? The snow coming toward us split, like a forked tongue, but only enough to save us for the next few minutes.

"Damn it. It isn't enough." Nuss cursed and pointed toward Zucker and Tau. "You keep her safe, you hear me. Even without the Land of Snowflakes power, she will still be strong enough to overcome the Mouse Queen."

Oh, no. I didn't like where that was going. "Don't you even think about sacrificing yourself for me again. I need you, I need all of you here with me."

Nuss ignored me and jumped up on his horse's

back, much wobblier than I liked. His balance was off without the use of both of his arms. I shouted to Zucker and Nuss. "Help him. Don't let him fall."

They both sped up and put themselves on either side of Nuss's horse so even if he fell, they could catch him. Their support didn't help even a little. Nuss jumped from his horse to the one carrying Fritz laid out across its back. If he was going to save the Fritz over himself, I was going to find a way to bring him back to life and then kill him.

But Nuss used his sword to nick the back of my brother's neck. Fritz squealed and I wanted to scream at him to shut up. The same shimmers of magic that had flowed from me, went up and along Nuss's sword. He once again pointed the tip at the snow and this time, it rumbled and tumbled and changed its path completely. The mass of it went around us, leaving the trail in front of us mostly debris free and safe.

It only took us a few more minutes to make it down to the edge of the Christmas tree forest where we could stop and look back at the destruction we'd avoided. I slipped down out of Leb's lap, and marched over to Nuss, yanking him down by the pantleg. "What the hell was that?"

Nuss hopped down and stepped away from me, looking down into the snow. "I told you it was a last resort."

Zucker and Tau joined us, boxing Nuss in. Zucker

poked him in the chest. "You drained magic from the Prince and Princess of the Land of Spirit and Magic to use for yourself. How, why?"

Nuss sighed and looked out over the crags of snow and rocks that could have killed us. "It is a secret long held by the Land of Snowflakes. You all see now why I've been so adamant that we do everything in our power to keep her safe."

He pointed to me, and I both wanted to kiss him again and slap him at the same time. Why was he keeping so many secrets from me?

Nuss continued on. "Had I known Fritz was here in the Winter Realm we would have had to rescue him too. The Mouse Queen can never get a hold of either of them. We'll be lucky if she doesn't already have some of his magic."

"Is this why you didn't want to touch me last night?" My bottom lip was still swollen from his harsh kiss, but it hurt less than where my thoughts were going.

Nuss swallowed hard and then knelt at my feet. He took my hand in his and gave it a soft kiss. "No, my lady. I want nothing more than to bond with you. But we must first find the crowns."

That meant we were headed straight to the Land of Snowflakes next because Nuss and I had some things to work out in and out of the bed. The siphoning my magic thing was high on the list. "What was that you said about me not needing the Land of Snowflakes power? Don't I need all the Lands?"

The four men looked at each other and did that silent communication thing that comes from knowing each other so well. Nuss answered for them all. "We don't know. It's not like the Winter Realm has ever lost an entire land and its royal family and been taken over by a power-hungry animal before. We hoped that by all of us bonding with you, we could grow your magic exponentially."

I'd assumed just Fritz and I were lost, not the whole land of Spirit and Magic that we'd been born to. Something niggled in my memory. "Drosselmeyer's stories must have mentioned something about this. Fritz, do you remember the stories of the Vivandiere and the seven crowns of the Winter Realm?"

Fritz wiggled around like a giant floppy fish, but Nuss had thoroughly tied him to the saddle, and he wasn't going anywhere. "Why would I? That was baby stuff."

"God, Fritz, don't be a dummy." I threw my hands up and rolled my eyes at him even though he couldn't see me. "Clearly it was all real."

"The realm might be real, but do you see a soldier woman traipsing around here? And if the Mouse Queen is so awful why hasn't the Vivandiere fought back herself?" Fritz's voice was beginning to grate on my nerves, as was his attitude.

But he had a point. Where was the Vivandiere? I turned to the men. "Are there legends or stories about what happened to her?"

"Who are you talking about, lass?" Leb was the last person I'd expect to keep secrets from me, so his question struck me as weird.

These were stories about their lands, they happened in their realm. I only knew them second-hand and had heard them as a child. "The soldier woman who hid all the pieces of the seven crowns from the wizard."

Nuss remained much too quiet and when we got to his land, he and I were having more than one conversation. I wasn't bonding with someone who didn't trust me.

"What about you two? Do the Fae lands keep secrets too?" I didn't think Zucker had held anything back from me. He'd been enthusiastic about everything from the first kiss.

"Subterfuge isn't the Sweet Fae way. But I don't know of a soldier woman called a Vivandiere. Tau?"

"I've got nothing. But perhaps the stories predate us. If that's so, the Fae Queens might know. They've both lived an exceptionally long time."

I'd been going on the assumption that I could find the pieces of the seven crowns because I knew all the stories of how and where they'd been hidden. But what if none of the stories were even real?

"How old are the Fae Queens?" Surely, they would remember. Or if they didn't, we'd find out just how much trouble we were in.

"Hundreds of your human years," Zucker said.

What? Hundreds? Let me get this straight in my

head. Fritz and I were born on the same day as all the men, so they were the same age as we were. Which was strange. They all seemed much older than me. But that must just be because they had so much more life experience than I did.

Drosselmeyer was at least twice as old as I was, probably three times. I didn't really know. He told Fritz and I the stories when we were young, but as if they happened in his lifetime. The Fae Queens were probably the same age or even younger than Drosselmeyer if they had sons my age. Mother Gingerbread didn't seem that old.

It couldn't be right that the stories were so old that they hadn't heard them or that my men were a hundred or more years older than I was. "I have a strange question. But does time move the same in the human realm as it does here?"

Tau shook his head. "No, vastly different and I'm sure that's been strange for you and Fritz to be caught in the middle of that. Sometimes, like now during the twelve days of Christmas we move much faster than the humans. One day here is like two hours there."

I've been in the Winter Realm a day, and only a few hours have passed at home? I'd be surprised if anyone even noticed I was gone. "At other times this world must pass the time slower because I think you all are older than I am, even though we're supposedly born on the same day."

Tau nodded confirming my suspicion. "Correct. But

very few residents of the realm are privy to information about the human world. Mostly only royalty."

I slapped my hand over my mouth to cover my sudden gasp. Because the men weren't the only ones who seemed to have a few years on me. I marched over to Fritz and slugged him in the tied-up arm. "You've been here before, a bunch of times, haven't you?"

"Ouch. Now who's the dummy, little sister?" Fritz squirmed around and glared at me.

"Oh, you still are. I can't believe you didn't tell me." I hit him again for good measure. Had to be the bit of warrior magic from the Gingerbread Kingdom in me feeling violent. If I didn't think he'd have valuable knowledge, that we could use, I'd shove him off this horse right now and tie him to a Christmas tree. My friends the pixies would feed him, so he didn't die.

"Oh shoot, we left Trost and Freunde in the Gingerbread Kingdom. Will they be okay with Mother Gingerbread?"

The pockets of my coat fluttered about and out popped my pixie friends. They buzzed around my face, flailing their arms, and making all kinds of sounds as if telling me all about their own adventure surviving the last hour in my pockets.

I laughed and held out my hands for them to land on. "When did you two hide in there and why didn't you come out before now?"

"They come when you call them, lass." Leb patted

Trost on the head. "Those are your Marzipan pixies. They've formed their own sort of bond with you."

"Mine? Like I own them?" They weren't pets, more like small people. "I don't like the thought of that. I don't want to own a person."

"No, no, yours in the same way we too belong to you. It's your magic and spirit that have them being loyal to you. They're as free as any other being in the Winter Realm to come and go as they please. Their pleasure is to serve you."

Aww. That had me feeling all gushy and mushy inside. "That I can do."

Zucker gave Trost a little twirl and they giggled. Then Freunde jumped onto my finger and swung back and forth like they were doing gymnastics. "Thank you for your friendship, little ones. I promise to cherish it always."

"You are such a sap, ClaraMarie. They're fricking servant fairies. You don't have to say thank you."

How was I even related to this schmoe? "Somebody punch him for me."

Both Zucker and Tau did exactly as I asked, and I enjoyed every one of Fritz's groans. "Thank you."

"Lass, we need to get a move on. The Mouse Queen's army will likely soon figure out you're not in the stronghold. I'd rather we had you safe in another Land where we have support before that happens."

Now to decide whether to go to the Fae Queens to

find out about the Vivandiere stories or to the Land of Snowflakes to dig into Nuss's secrets. But if I had to find the Snowflake crown and the stories weren't true, it didn't do us any good to go there. I didn't like either choice.

BIG ROCK CANDY MOUNTAIN

ZUCKER

a black line of mice snaked its way down the side of the mountain. I thought we'd have more time, but Konig was a crafty bastard at best and a ruthless general at worst. We were getting his worst today. I pulled one of my daggers from the sheath and pointed it up the quagmire of snow. "Nuss, can you do your magic trick again to bring another avalanche down on them?"

"Not without hurting Clara or the Prince."

Tau drew his bow and let off three arrows in one shot. They flew straight and far and struck the head of the column of mouse soldiers. "If we hurry, we can get to the edge of the Sweet Fae lands. We can hide in the border's glamour."

"I don't know what that means, but if it means not being eaten alive by mice again, I'm in." Princess Clara ran back toward her horse and Leb had to sprint to keep up with her. We took off in a dead run for the border of the Gingerbread Kingdom and the Land of Sweets. But we would be exposed until we hit the Fae magic that the uninitiated got lost in. Konig would have a tough time getting through, but he'd know exactly where we went.

I directed us toward the nearby line of trees. "If we skirt the edge of the Christmas Tree Forest the army won't attack the pixies and won't know which land we've headed for."

Clara looked horrified at the idea. "You're sure? Won't or can't."

Nuss glanced behind us and gave his horse a nudge to put on some speed. "No one has issue with the Land of Comfort and Joy. They are and have always been neutral and the Christmas Tree Forest neutral ground."

"How many wars have you guys had?" The Princess was getting a fast initiation into the politics of the Winter Realm.

"A few." Most were long since forgotten, but not the schism between the Fae lands. That caused generations of discord between our people. I never thought I'd get to introduce Tau to my family. Clara was making that possible. Probably.

I had to keep the hope alive that her presence would keep him safe from any angry Sweet Fae who had long memories and weren't quick to forgive the past. Like my mother.

We slipped into the cover of the forest and made a quick turn toward the border with my homeland.

The magic of anticipation danced across my skin and into my blood. We were headed to the Land of Sweets, and I'd been gone for far too long. I could hardly wait to show off the Prince and Princess of my heart. My mother always said I fell in love too fast. She wasn't entirely correct. Lust, sure, but love?

No. I'd only ever been in love with one person until Princess Clara. But to the Queen of Sweets' point, I'd fallen in love with both her and Tau at first sight. Tau had taken me far too long to seduce. But sweet Clara was as sensual as any Sugar Fae, and half the anticipation running through me was hers.

The rest was from a preternatural sense that I'd developed over the years. We were finally going to find the broken piece of the seven crowns that represented the Land of the Sweets. I'd already had a taste of Clara's magic last night and knew it would be all the more sweeter once I could bond with her.

The only thing that would make it even better was if Tau and I could bond with her together. Then perhaps I'd find out what he was holding back from me. He wanted love. I loved him. But he wasn't wrong when he said it would fill in something missing when Clara was between us.

The tingle of the glamour whooshed over me as

I led our band out of the forest and into the snowy hills of the Land of Sweets. The Fae guard would feel our arrival and descend upon us soon. I stopped and waited for the rest to come through and put myself on one side of Tau. I gave him a look of concern and he nodded, gravely understanding the threat he was under just by being here with us.

He pulled his quiver with his bow and arrows from his chest and buckled it to the saddle behind him to show himself to be unarmed. Leb slowed his stallion so that he and Clara rode to one side of Tau and I on the other. Nuss moved in front making a shield around Tau.

They all remembered our first days together in the Guard when Tau and I were at each other's throats. Hate sex was almost as good as bonding. But that was back when I was the one who didn't entirely believe we'd ever find the missing princess.

"Halt in the name of Queen SugarPlum." A Sweet Fae guard shouted from his hiding place in the glamour. We all slowed our horses and I held up my hands and nodded at the others to do the same. Sweet Fae guards were lethal assassins who wouldn't hesitate to kill unwelcomed visitors.

"I know I've been gone a long time, but surely you recognize your own Prince." I let my silver hair down from the tie keeping it out of my face as we rode and let my Fae aura shine. The purple light spread into the glamour, revealing six Sweet Fae guards with their swords trained on us.

"Prince Zucker? Is it truly you?" They descended on us and had their blades at the throats of Nuss, Tau, and Leb in an instant. "Who are these strangers with you? Have you been coerced into letting them into our lands? Say the word and we will free you and your lovely captive companion."

"Hey, I could be a threat too, you know. How do you know I'm not some—"

I cut Clara off before she could get us all into more trouble. "Ladies, gentleman, allow me to introduce you to Princess Clara from the Land of Spirit and Magic."

They collectively gasped and I had to hold in a chuckle. Mostly because I understood exactly how they felt. I was still flabbergasted she was here, even more so that she was soon to be my spirit mate.

Clara waved and made eyes at them all. "Hi. Nice to meet you. Please take your swords off my, umm, friends', throats."

The ones by Nuss and Leb stepped back, but the one with her sword to Tau, glowered. "Surely you don't claim this Flower Fae."

I was about to say something, but Clara reached out her hand and put two fingers on the Fae Guard's blade. She pushed the tip down and away. "I do. We aren't yet bonded, but he is mine, just the same as Zucker, Nuss, and Leb are. Kindly, back the fuck off."

Oh, sweet Christmas star, her newfound warrior

magic was going to be the death of us. But damn, I found her dirty mouth hot and couldn't wait until she let me slide my cock between her lips.

To my absolute surprise, the Fae guard dropped her sword and gave Clara a small bow. "Yes, my lady. If you're sure."

"I'm sure. But I do appreciate your fierce determination to protect me and your prince. I'm rather found of him too." Clara gave the guard a wink, entirely charming every Fae here.

If Tau and I didn't already have a claim on her, she'd have no end of lovers wanting to warm her bed while she was here in the land of the Sweets. I was even sure I saw a bit of pink on the cheeks of the guard Clara had engaged with, and I'd never known a tough Fae guard like her to blush.

"Please follow us, my lady, my liege." The guards formed a phalanx both in front and behind us. They may have ceded to Clara, but they didn't entirely trust Tau.

I hated how stiff he now sat in his seat and wanted nothing more than to wrap and arm around him and pepper him with kisses. I needed the assurance he was okay probably more than he needed it from me. Regardless, tonight I was getting him into my bed. Even better if Clara was between us.

"Zucker, what is that?" Clara pointed to a candy cane vine fluttering with peppermint butterflies. Then she pointed to a candy floss bush, and then over to a maple sugar tree.

Her delicious innocence at experiencing the wonders of the Winter Realm had every instinct to protect her from the harsh realities of our world bubbling up like hot caramel. "Welcome the Land of Sweets. We're the main provider of foodstuffs for the realm because of our rich natural resources."

I plucked a sugary leaf from the maple tree and held it up to her lips. Her tongue poked out giving the point a taste and my cock went from my usual ready at any moment half-mast to ready to throw her to the ground and fuck her in the snow, instantly.

"Mmm. That's yummy. But do you all only eat sweets? I think my teeth are going to rot out of my head."

Tau laughed. "I think you'll find most of the Sweet Fae are sugar addicts."

His joviality was cut short by the blockade in front of the gates to SugarPlum castle. The Sweet Fae Queen in all her glory, surrounded by a whole host of guards, weapons pointed at us, stood directly in front of the only entrance to the gates around the castle and its grounds.

"No friend of the Sweet Fae would bring such rabble into my house. What are your intentions?" The magic of her charm and raw sexuality wafted through the air, wrapping itself around everyone, including the guards until they were all so enamored with her that their tongues hung out. I alone was immune.

"Hello, mother. Pull your allure back a bit, will you? I'd like to introduce you to the Princess of Spirit and Magic." I motioned to Clara and noted that she too was unaffected by my mother's charms. Interesting.

The Queen raised an eyebrow and did her best to look even more intimidating than she already was. Clara blinked a few times and smiled back. An entire lifetime's worth of emotions flickered through my mother's eyes as she measured up the princess.

I had absolutely no idea which way she would decide. My mother hadn't ever put much credence into the Christmas Star prophecy and never understood why I wanted to join the Nutcracker guard in the first place. She'd be content for the Mouse Queen to run amok throughout the rest of the lands as long as they still bought our sweets and stayed out of our lands.

I wanted more for the Fae.

That same tingle of anticipation danced across my skin and psyche as I held my breath waiting for the assessment of the one woman, besides Clara, that I'd ever given a damn about. If my mother decided she didn't want to have anything to do with Clara, we'd have a challenging time searching for the broken crown of the Sweet Fae. But with her blessing, would come all the strength of her army behind our mission.

"I like her, you may enter." She gave a little flick of her fingers and the sex magic snapped back, releasing everyone from her spell. She scowled at the guards closest to her and shooed them away. "Go, get, go, you silly Sweets. We've got a celebration to plan to welcome home my son."

I didn't miss that she left off the part of welcoming my friends. She may have approved of Clara, but it would take more than a smile to get Tau into her good favor. I'd rather not have to choose between the two of them, but I would, and Tau would win every day all day, twice on Sundays.

We dismounted and I took Clara's hand to lead her though the gates. I reached for Tau's as well, but he shook his head and fell in line behind us.

Clara worried her lip between her teeth. "I don't think your mother liked me very much."

"It's me she doesn't like, Princess," Tau said very matter of factly. "But I can live with that as long as you have my heart and I yours."

Wait, was that line meant for me or Clara? Damn it. I didn't care what anyone in the Land of Sweets thought, not even my mother. I whipped around, putting Clara between the two of us, and grabbed the back of Tau's neck to pull him close. I gave him a hot and hard kiss. I'd put Clara between us to keep her protected and so she wouldn't think she wasn't a part of this but wanted to grind my hard cock against Tau too. I needed him to know it was more than my body he had claim to.

Tau broke the kiss before me, but he wasn't unaffected. "I know."

"Just so we're clear." I searched his eyes, willing him to understand exactly how important he and his heart were to me.

Clara eyes were as wide as dessert bowls and her breathing was soft, but fast. Her magic surged up between the three of us and made the embrace feel like a warm hug that could turn into something so much more. As soon as we found that crown it would. Nobody said I couldn't fuck the sugar out of both of them while we were looking for it.

"I'm fairly sure everyone here gets it now. But can we move along? My arse is sore from riding all day and your Queen said something about a party, where I hope you've got some of that famous Sugar Plum cider, but any old ale will do." We three looked over at Leb, who had pulled his acts out and was tapping the broadside of it against his hand.

Uh-oh. Nuss stepped in front of us and pulled his sort out as well. He jerked his chin toward the gathering crowd of Sweet Fae, most of whom had menacing scowls on their faces.

My mother turned around, looked at the three of us in our embrace and at the fae staring at us disapprovingly. She rolled her eyes, shook her head, lifted her layers of flowing skirts so they weren't her way and marched back down the walkway to us.

Oh, fuck. Here we go. I knew there'd be backlash to

my actions. I thought I was prepared. I squeezed my lovers in my arms and then turned to face her. She got within two inches of me, stopped, looked me dead in the eye and that's when I knew.

She might be a fierce Sweet Fae warrior who was feared by most everyone in the Land, but she, above all, believed in the magic of love. In a move I never thought I'd see the Sugar Plum Queen make, she put her hand on Tau's cheek and patted it. Then she repeated our words. "Just so we're clear. I know too."

Then she clapped her hands, to get the onlookers attention, as if she didn't already have it and let her voice and her allure project through them all. "You all are much better looking with smiles on your faces rather than scowls. Change those faces or feel my wrath."

The Queen of the Sweet Fae whipped right back around and continued her march toward the castle, while we all stared after her.

"Man, I wouldn't want to be on your mother's bad side," Clara said.

I'd worried for a long time that I wouldn't ever be in my mother's good graces, that she wouldn't accept me because of who I loved. I hadn't been home in far too long because of this mission and my fervent relationship with Tau. The relief of knowing the Queen was my true ally, flowed through my heart like a river of the sweetest plum syrup. "No, nor me. But I would for the two of you."

"Hey, what are we?" Leb waved his hand between himself and Nuss. "Chopped nuts?"

I had a quick remark about something I'd like to do two Nuss's nuts, but held it in. It had become hard for any of us to express how we felt about the others in our brotherhood, sense Koenig's betrayal.

Instead of saying something smart I gave Nuss an eyebrow waggle and he returned it with his usual eyeroll. He clapped Leb on the arm. "Yes, my Viking friend, that is exactly what we are."

I did love them both, but not in the same way as I did Tau and Clara. They knew and understood that, or at least I thought they did.

Perhaps once we were all bonded with the princess it would be easier for me to express what was in my heart. Just the act of thinking that had me wondering if that was Tau's reticence too.

The sooner we could find the Sweet Fae and the Flower Fae crowns the better. First, we had to attend this welcoming party and hopefully survive long enough to convince the rest of the Sugar Plum court and our people to open their hearts as my mother had. Not everyone would fall in line just because she told them too.

Our guards kept close as we walked the rest of the way to the castle. When we reached the gates, I directed the guards to take Prince Friedrich to secured area. I wished we had a dungeon to throw him in, but locked rooms would have to do until we could figure out what to do with him.

Trumpets sounded and Clara gasped as we walked forward into the castle's courtyard, decorated in colorful banners abuzz with Marzipan pixies. Never let it be said that the Fae were ever unprepared for a party. The courtyard was already filling with revelers, piles of food, and every Sweet Fae's favorite, a dance floor.

Clara's pixies appeared from the depths of her furry cloak and buzzed around her head. She laughed and held out her hand for them to land on. "I think they're asking if they can go play with their friends."

"That's about the gist of it. Marzipan pixies go crazy for a party. They love very little more."

"Off you go then. See you soon, you two." Her pixies flitted away, and each brought back a treat for Clara to try. Freunde brought a mug of rich, dark coffee, and Trost brought some sugared fruits. "Oh, you didn't have to bring these to me, but thank you so much."

Those pixies loved when she was so open with her gratitude. Most of us took them for granted and I'd have to try harder to be more gracious of our little friends and the way they loved to feel helpful.

Clara tried each of the treats the pixies brought over, and we made our way into the party. When we got to the dance floor, she stopped and stared. There was a longing in her eyes that had my insides clenching.

"I hope you know how to dance, Princess." I pointed

out the dance floor and the merrymakers already doing a few steps around the edges.

Clara stopped and stared. "Dance? You want me to dance?"

"I want to dance with you, love." I could hardly wait to hold her in my arms and let the magic inside of her free.

DANCE OF THE SUGAR PLUM FAIRY

CLARA

*F*or the two whole days that I had been in the Winter Realm, all I had experienced was war. I wasn't even sure if anyone in this place knew how to do anything but fight. Well, and have super amazing sex. Maybe it was because the first people that we visited were the gingerbread Vikings and they were clearly built for battle.

The Sweet Fae we'd met so far looked more ready to eat my face off than throw a party, but that's exactly what was happening. It took me months of planning, calling caterers, getting in a tree and a professional decorator, cleaning the main floor of the house, sending out invitations, and a million other preparations to throw our annual Christmas Eve party. The

Sugar Plum Queen put this feast, with an entire symphony, and dancing together in, what, like thirty minutes.

"Come, Princess of Spirit and Magic and let me look at you." The Queen pulled my hand away from Zucker's and had me doing a little twirl for her. "You are quite beautiful, I can see why my Zucker is taken with you. But your dress is a bit in tatters. That just won't do."

She clapped her hands, and a dozen ballerinas in every color, shape, and size, dressed in fluffy pink tutus surrounded me in an instant forming a wall around us. They fussed over me, with someone pinning up my hair, another patting my face with powder, and a half dozen of them with hands flying over my dress and fabric whooshing around me. I almost felt as if I was caught up in a bippity-boppity-boo of a fairy godmother.

I honestly never even felt my dress come off, and I was never naked, but within a few moments and a lot of squeals, I was in a similar outfit to the women around me. Except the bodice of mine was encrusted with sparkling jewels, and the skirt was covered in an intricate hand-embroidered design. I even had pointe-shoe-like slippers on, with ribbons beautifully wrapped around my ankles. They were pretty, but there was no way I'd be able to walk around in them all night.

The Sugar Plum Queen tipped her head to one side. "Go on, try them out."

My toes weren't taped, I didn't have my little lamb-swool half socks to cushion, and I'd be tumbling over in pain within a millisecond, but I did as she asked. The Queen wasn't someone to say no to. I took a couple of steps, and it was as if these were my own pointe shoes from my bag at home. The elastic and ribbons were cut to the exact right length and everything.

I popped up onto the points and tip tapped a few steps. Someone had already banged the toes out, so they weren't overly loud and there was just the right amount of support in the box. I couldn't believe how comfortable they were. It was like dancing on clouds, or puffs of cotton candy.

This was the most fun dancing I'd ever had and all I'd only taken a few steps. I did an extra twirl and landed right in Zucker's arms. "You're a fucking gorgeous dancer, Princess. Shall we?"

Oh goodness. Tittering about was fun, but to do a real dance with a danseur? I'd never. No one ever wanted to be partnered up with me.

The other ballerinas clapped and took up positions all around the edge of the dancefloor, ready to support the leading role, I'd apparently just been cast in. I glanced over at the Queen, and she gave me a nod of encouragement.

What in the world would have happened if I hadn't been trained in dance? It was clearly a part of their culture and expected of me. God, I hoped I didn't make a fool out of myself.

I dragged my feet. "I look ridiculous in this costume. I'm like a parade float."

"I don't know what a parade float is, but I assure you that ridiculous is not what you are. I on the other hand have a ridiculously hard cock just thinking about getting to dance with you, and if you'll notice so does every Sugar Fae man here."

I glanced around the gathering of Zucker's people, and he was right. Every man had a bulge in the front of their pants, and some were even stroking themselves. A few were partnered up with other men or women and they were, umm, enjoying each other's bodies too.

"This isn't a giant sex party or something, is it?" I was just getting used to the idea of bonding through sex with more than one man. I wasn't doing it in front of a crowd.

The other thing I noticed this time around was that none of the women here had that tall, ultra-thin body of a ballerina. Yet, they all looked like beautiful dancers to me.

Most of them had bodies similar in shape to mine. Thick thighs, a belly, a big round bottom, and actual breasts that filled out the front of their costumes. Was this why I was curvy yet still felt drawn to dance? Even the Queen was lush and round, just like Mother Gingerbread had been.

I couldn't quite fathom that kind of dissonance from the world I grew up in that told me that a larger body wasn't meant to be a ballerina or a soldier.

"Later tonight, I'll explain in more detail the intricacies of the Fae's sexual culture. We are much freer with the pleasures of the flesh than say the Lan of Snowflake, and apparently the human realm." He winked at me, and took a place beside me, holding out a hand to begin the dance. "But don't worry, this isn't an orgy. Those are only for special occasions."

"You're a tease." Which I was starting to like very much.

"Anticipation is half the fun, my lady." Instead of starting us in a traditional stance, he pulled me to him, and wrapped one hand around my waist and held my other up as if we were going to waltz instead of perform a Grande pas de duex. "Ready?"

"Zucker," I didn't want to screw up what seemed like an important moment. "I don't know the choreography. I can't just go out here and dance."

He ignored my protest and led me to center stage. "The dance will come from your spirit, pretty princess. Every Winter Realm borne has that inside of them. I promise you'll know what to do."

Zucker bent his head and pressed his mouth to mine, parted my lips with his tongue and the magic inside of me sparkled to life. I heard oohs and ahhs from the audience directed at us but was too caught up in this kiss to care. I lifted myself up onto my toes, deepening the kiss and putting my hand on Zucker's shoulder, ready to let the magic flow through me and into the steps of the dance.

There were more joyful exclamations and clapping, and when I opened my eyes, swirls of colorful snowflakes spun around us, showing me exactly how and where to take my steps. It was just as Zucker had said. My spirit was guiding me, and I knew what to do without even having to learn someone else's choreography or practice any routine.

The tinkling celeste music binked and bopped as if timed to my little bourrée steps. Do do do, do, do, do, doodle-loodle-loo. Zucker followed along as my cavalier and we floated to one side of the stage, me up on my toes on pointe, and back down again. My hands and fingers flowed, chasing the streams of magic, on their spinning path. I reached for them, performing my absolute best arabesques, kicking my leg gracefully up into the air. I'd study dance for so long and knew the names and mechanics for each and every move, but in this moment none of that mattered. It was only the music and the story I was telling through the motions of each lift of my foot, each flick of my wrist.

These moves made me feel more beautiful than ever. More so than the time I'd tried on my wedding dress. How far away that seemed now. I was in a different place and time, and while I'd felt like a fairy princess that day, it was nothing compared to dancing for the gathered crowd of Sweet Fae.

All eyes were on me, and I wasn't the least bit uncomfortable with them all watching. It was as if this was the one role I'd ever meant to be cast in. The reason I'd never fit any other part. This one was here waiting for me.

I followed the magic around in a long oval piqué manège, stepping and spinning, running my hands through the sparkles, darting over mystical obstacles with quick, fast coupé jeté jumps. While the dance was exhilarating, my energy was starting to flag. But I could see the finale of where the swirls of magic were leading me, so I pushed until I was almost there. Zucker bounded his way to where I would end the dance, and Tau leaped in next to him. I gave a final Chasse up, where they both lifted me into the air, one under each shoulder, holding me above the crowd and spun me in a grand finale.

When they brought me back down to earth from my flight among the angels, I was breathing hard and feeling the glow of the most thrilling moment of my life. The Fae around us clapped and cheered. Even Nuss and Leb were applauding and staring at me like I was their absolute pride and joy.

"Princess, this performance won't be forgotten by the Sugar Plum Court for an awfully long time. What a way to demonstrate the way to the lost broken piece of the crown here in the Land of Sweets."

We all took bows which gave me a moment to consider what Zucker had just said. We turned and bowed to the other side of the stage, and I still wasn't sure what he meant.

"I'm not sure what you mean. I was just following

the magic, like you said. My spirit guided me through the steps."

"I suppose from inside of the dance, you couldn't see the magical glamours around you, but the rest of us could." Tau wiped a bead of sweat from my upper lip and stared down at my mouth. "It's why I had to join at the end."

The Fae around us hadn't stopped cheering and were gathering around us on the stage. Nuss and Leb pushed their way through the throng of people to get to us. The four of them boxed me in and took a step forward to lead me off the dance floor.

"Wait." I held up my hands and didn't move an inch. "What are you two on about. What did you see that I didn't?" I thought I was just following the spirit and the magic like Zucker said I would. Now they tell me there was some kind of show going on around me?

Tau had been watching from the sidelines until the very end of the performance. "Your dance and the projections of the glamour showed you following a path from the Sugar Plum castle through the Fae lands and finding a crown."

Zucker nodded and smiled down at me sending a whole rush of butterflies whizzing from my belly and between my legs. He was as excited as the rest of his people, and I was caught up in it. "That's why everyone is cheering. You've revealed where the broken piece of the Sweet Fae crown is and now we can retrieve it."

Tau looked between the two of us. There was something more and I could almost feel his trepidation coursing out of him. I put my hand on his arm and he calmed a little. A zip of the excitement from Zucker went through me and met the zing of Tau's worry, melding the two of them together into something calmer.

They both took a deep breath and met each other's eyes, and I was swept up into a different kind of magic flowing between the three of us. Tau cleared his throat and broke the spell. No, not broke it, the zips and zings of this connection was stronger than ever, and it had my chest fluttering. But Tau was worried about something. "Your path showed you going all the way to the border between the Land of Sweets and the Land of Flowers."

"Yes," Zucker said, agreeing, but with a note of confusion in his voice. "Do you not want us to journey that close to Flower Fae lands? If my family can accept you, is there not hope that yours will welcome me too?"

Tau gave the slightest shake of his head. "I wish I could say that they would. I was raised to hate you and everything about the Sweet Fae. You know how long it took me to give in to the attraction between us."

I waited for Zucker to scowl or darkness to cloud his eyes. Instead, he grinned that cocky smile that made me giddy and more than ready to find the crown and bond with him. "Then I'll just have to seduce the rest of your Land the same as I did you and make them all fall in love with me."

Tau rolled his eyes and shook his head, but he smiled too. That was apparently the right thing for Zucker to say. Love was high on Tau's priority list and my own heart went melty because of that. No one back home had ever thought falling in love was important, especially not for me.

The Winter Realm was giving me the chance to fall in love not just with one man, or even four or five, but also with myself.

I took both Tau and Zucker's hands in mine and brought them together over my heart. "If the Flower Fae have learned to hate, we'll be the ones to show them how much more powerful love is."

The Sugar Plum Queen pushed her way into our circle and grabbed my hand from the two of them. "If anyone can do it, it's the Court of Steel Tree, but you'd better hurry. We just caught a mouse at the border trying to get in."

Where the hell was the Vivandiere when we needed her?

SUGAR, FLOWER, SOLDIER, SPY

TAU

onig was fucking relentless. Granted, since the prize was princess Clara, we all were. I'd do anything for the magic of her love.

My own people had almost turned their backs on me when I joined the Nutcracker guard. The only way I had convinced of the DewDrop court that I needed to serve alongside the other lands was when the Mouse Queen had let her rodent army loose on our fields. The devastation had nearly caused civil War within our own land.

Not everyone had such fear and loathing of the other, especially when we didn't have enough food to feed every man, woman, and child, but the Sweet Fae did.

But the ones who did hate, who didn't want to take any help, would be the ones guarding the border. "If the cave we saw Clara enter in the dance is where I think it is..."

I wasn't ready to say it out loud. I didn't want to get everyone's hopes up that we could possibly find two pieces of broken crowns at the same time. because finding both the Sweet Fae and the Flower Fae crowns would mean our two peoples had been fighting for the wrong reasons since the beginning.

I redirected my attention on Clara. Her emotions were all of wonder and hope, and I needed them to feed my spirit. There were so many intense emotions pushing at my consciousness and it was hard to tell the difference between those of the people around me and my own. It had been a long time since any of us had been at such a large gathering of people.

Since the beginning of the rebellion, it had mostly just been the four of us, recruiting more residents of the winter realm to the underground resistance, and fighting back in small groups. The sooner we left on this quest for the Sweet Fae crown the better. "You won't be able to enter the cave we saw in your dance without both of us."

Zucker crossed arms and nodded gravely. I irritatingly found old prejudices against the Sugar Plum Court bubbling up inside. If he was familiar with where this cave was, and so was I, we both had more knowledge of each other's lands than the average Fae. Which likely meant that Zucker had spied in my land in his youth, just as I had in Sweet Fae lands.

Why was I the one being suspicious, and he only thinking of our mission? I'd blame that on the swirl of emotions all around us. Not the ones buzzing around inside my own chest.

"Okay." She waved her hand between the four of us. "I sort of thought we'd all go there together anyway."

Nuss narrowed his eyes and shook his head. "I hoped we'd at least have one night of peace here. I'll go on the offensive and keep Konig distracted while the rest of you go find that broken piece of the crown."

Leb grabbed the back of Nuss's shirt to stop him from moving. "Oh no you don't. You're not getting out of being there when Zucker and Clara bond. Good try."

Clara bit her lip, trying to keep the hurt in her heart from showing on her face. It didn't work. Nuss took one look at her and went from determined to horrified.

"No, I... Clara, I swear to you, I'm only trying to protect you."

While we were all training to find and protect her, we should have given Nuss some lessons in protecting her heart too. Or fucking being around a woman at all. When the hell had he gotten so damn awkward?

"Then come help me retrieve this crown. I promise I won't make you join the bonding. I don't ever want you to do something you're not ready to."

All right. Now I wanted to kick Nuss's ass. What I was going to do was make sure he was watching every single minute of the consummation of the bond between Clara and Zucker, and then the same when she and I bonded too. I'd admit I was mad at him for not joining us in bringing her pleasure. Stupid Snowflake and his stupid religion.

But maybe the dumbass had actually learned a lesson. He stepped up to Clara, lifted her chin and stared into her eyes with so much want and need pouring off him, I could practically taste it. He licked his lips and I swear he was going to kiss her. But of course, he controlled himself. "I think that's what I'm supposed to be saying to you."

The Sugar Plum Queen cleared her throat, but it took Nuss and Clara a moment to break their gazes from each other. "While I'm the last fairy to tell you to get a room, perhaps you could restrain yourselves from until we can get you out of the castle and on your quest to find the crown?"

If we didn't get him naked during the next couple of bonding's I'd be surprised. Even the stoic Nutcracker Captain could only hold out for so long. Nuss still didn't step away and I was about to shove the two of them together just to relieve the tension.

"I swear to the Christmas star, we should have gone to the Land of Snowflakes for your piece of the broken crown. But since we didn't, you're going to have to keep your dick hard a little longer. Now, let's get—"

A burst of emotion, a craving deep need, hit my psyche like a punch to the gut, taking me almost to my knees, and stealing my breath with its intensity.

Zucker grabbed me under the arm to steady me. "What is it?"

"The mouse army..." my voice creaked out, "they're inside the barrier to the Sweet Fae lands, and Konig is with them."

Clara's face paled and then her cheeks lit up like pink petunias. She was trying hard to bank her feelings. Toward Konig.

She was fucking attracted to him.

I'd never wanted to forsake the empathic gift I had before. I'd worked for years to hone the small amount of magic that came with being Fae, but in this moment, I wish I didn't know how she felt at all. Clara didn't know him like the rest of us. She only saw him as the dashing captain of the opposing army.

The rest of the guard were more focused on me, and I wouldn't give up her secret just yet. Once she and I were bonded and her magic amplified my gifts for her use, she would see the real Mouse Prince for what he really was. A traitor.

The sooner we got her away from him, the better. "Zucker, your majesty, you're not going to like that I know this, but I promise when it's all over we'll figure how to deal with what I'm about to say."

The Queen gave me one raised eyebrow. "Go on."

If we were in the Land of Flowers, and I was Zucker... no, I couldn't think like that. The Sugar Plum Queen had accepted me. It was another step toward peace between our people. Clara's spirit and magic would be the leap forward we needed. A leap we wouldn't be able to make if we couldn't get out of the castle and find that crown. "I apologize in advance, your majesty. You should close the castle up tight, draw up the bridge and make this the fortress I know it to be."

Zucker shook his head as if what I was saying was no big deal. "Everyone knows Sugar Plum castle is ready for battle."

Yeah, but few knew this next part. I lowered my voice so only the six of us would hear. "And we should escape into the peppermint caves through your network of tunnels beneath the castle."

The queen closed her eyes and took a long breath. "I could make you forget you ever knew that, but I won't if you promise to bring me the sugared head of the Mouse Queen."

None should ever make the mistake of forgetting the Sugar Plum Queen was primarily a warrior queen. Clara stared hard at Zucker's mother and tipped her head in that cute thinking thing that she did. "You aren't by any chance the Vivandiere, are you?"

The queen eyed Clara with a new appreciation. "Who told you about her?"

"A story-teller from the human realm." That's all she

said. The curiosity of all the rest of us was palpable in the air around us.

The queen looked over her shoulder as if she was worried someone else might be listening. "I am not the Vivandiere, but I will tell you this. The stories are all true."

"I knew it." These were the answers Clara had been seeking and we didn't have any more time. "Where is she now? Why isn't she here to help fight against the Mouse Queen?"

I sucked in a sharp breath as another wave of Konig's emotions struck me. He wasn't just here to for a battle, he was here for Clara. "We have to go, now."

Leb picked Clara up and pushed his way through the crowd toward the towers of the castle, opening a way for the rest of us to follow. "One of these days we are going to quit running and bring the fight to that bastard."

"We will," Nuss held out his arms to hold back the revelers that knew nothing of the approaching army. "Once we have the crowns and can rightfully take back the throne."

Zucker went next. "Shit. Mother, I've had the guards put the Prince of Spirit and Magic in the south rooms. He's in league with the Mouse Queen. See what you can find out from him about—"

"Holy sugary snowflakes. Go, already. I'll take care of the stinking traitorous prince."

I wasn't sure if she meant Friedrich or the Mouse Prince. Both, if we were lucky.

I sprinted ahead of Leb and into the first tower. While I'd only ever been in the tunnels and caves outside the castle, the schematics of the building itself were seared into my mind. Zucker joined me an opened a big wooden door before I had to reveal exactly how much I knew about his home. Someday I would have to come clean.

The room he led us into looked like a very average sitting room, with a whole host of plush chairs, antique tables, and tapestries all decorated in sweets, desserts, and sugary treat motifs. I'd laugh, but the DewDrop castle was just as decked out with flowers and other flora.

Zucker grabbed the edge of a wall-length tapestry and pulled the bottom half away from the wall. If I didn't know there was a hidden door there, I never would have guessed. The whole thing was expertly painted to look like the stones around it. "None of you ever saw this."

He pushed against the stones and they sunk back, then popped open, revealing the secret passageway. Just inside, was a cache of weapons which I was thankful for because it included a quiver with arrows and a bow. I slipped the quiver over my shoulder and tested the tip of an arrow. Sharp. Good, because we might need them.

"Oh, my giddy aunt. This is all very cloak and dagger fabulous." Clara ducked under Zucker's arm and into the darkness.

I followed next and took her hand. I let the flower power inside of me that gave me a sparkling green aura push up and out of me, and the hallway lit up enough for us to see our way forward. Leb and Nuss followed me and soon Zucker's purple aura added its light from behind. The passageway sloped down in long spirals until we were well below the castle grounds. We stopped at the bottom, where the tunnels split off into six different directions.

"How do you know where to go from here?" Clara asked, looking around the darkness.

Zucker came forward and pointed to some symbols carved into the walls. "Each tunnel takes us toward one of the other Lands. The axe for the Gingerbread Kingdom, the snowflake for the Land of Snowflakes and so on. We'll go this way."

He pointed down the tunnel marked with the flower. Clara hesitated and stared at the other arches in the stone. She pointed to a spot that had been scratched over, obliterating the symbol beneath. The tunnel went even more silent as we all swallowed our next breaths.

"Is it someplace bad?" Clara whispered.

I pulled one of the arrows from the quiver on my back and forfeited the sharp arrowhead. I scratched the symbol that had represented the Land of Spirit and Magic, an elongated eight-pointed star with a wisp flowing behind it, that now reminded me of the way our princess looked when she danced, curvy and elegant. When I was finished, Clara stepped closer and ran her fingers over the mark.

"This is for the Land of Spirit and Magic, isn't it?"

I nodded.

"No one goes there anymore?"

"There isn't anywhere to go. Your Kingdom was destroyed long ago."

"No." She shook her head and tipped it to the side looking down the dark hallway. "I don't think that's right. There is definitely something still there. I can feel it, right here."

Clara took my hand and placed it against her chest. Magic, just like that which we felt last night during the consummation of her bonding with Leb tingled across my knuckles. She reached her other arm out toward the rest of the guard. "Each of you, give me your hands."

One by one they put their hands on top of and beside mine. Swirls of magic lifted off her skin and lit up the darkness even brighter than either of our Fae auras. Leb groaned and Nuss closed his eyes. Zucker looked at me and I could read the heat in them.

"We have to go there." Clara took a step forward, breaking our contact with her. The spell faded, and the tunnel went pitch black once again.

Clara gulped back a sob and turned, throwing

herself into me and Zucker. Her sadness tasted like wolfsbane, it was so strong and pungent. "I promise, my lady. We four will do everything in our power to help you reclaim your land. But the first step to that is finding the broken crowns."

THE MOUSE CROWN

KONIG

$\mathcal{T}$he Nutcrackers thought they could escape me, but the longer I was near her, the connection between Princess Clara grew tighter. I'd been able to use my shifter senses to track her, but the moment I kissed her in the Christmas Tree Forest, I didn't need those anymore. It was as if there was a magical tether between us.

That connection had grown taught when they'd escaped into the Sweet Fae lands. I'd set my ambush at the border of the border of the Land Snowflakes, assuming that's where Nuss would want to take her next. How the fool had simply sat there and watched when the others had joined in the bonding was nothing less than I expected. But I knew what his people had riding on him finding their crown and their subsequent bonding.

I should have set up a contingency plan for the fae borders. They were smart to use the glamour there to deter my army. But Zucker and Tau weren't the only ones with good spy craft. My spies were practically undetectable when they were in mouse form and had discovered the ancient tunnel system beneath Sugar-Plum castle used as escape routes long ago. I kept that information to myself for when I needed it.

This was exactly where I'd lay my trap. It didn't take much to figure out that this is where they'd go when my army attacked the castle where they celebrated their escape from me.

There was more than one way to catch a princess. I'd much rather have her come to me willingly. That would be much more devastating for the rest of the Guard.

I shifted into my mouse form and pushed my way through the fae glamour. No one took notice of a single mouse scurrying around a party filled with people and food. I watched in awe as Clara danced. Her magic was so much more than any of the rest of them understood. Being here in her presence loosened the binds of not being close to her that felt wrapped around my chest when I couldn't be near her.

All the more reason I needed her to see the atrocities this war had wrought on the Land of Animals. She could never be bound to me in the same way she was to Leb, but that didn't mean I didn't have my ways of making her do what was right.

Before her performance was even finished, I called to the mouse army to begin the attack on the Sugar-Plum court. Then I scurried into the castle, counting on Zucker and Tau to use them to escape. There would be no other option.

Ah, here they were now. Into the tunnels they went, not for a moment noticing me hiding in the shadows and debris following along. I relished being so close to the princess while I could. Her magic warmed even my cold spirit.

I'd have to be very careful not to fall in love with her. She was a means to an end. That didn't mean I wouldn't enjoy fucking her until she fell in love with me.

The party paused at the junction where the tunnels split off toward the other lands. My army was ready to shift to any of the exits. Except of course the one that led to the land of Spirit and Magic. No one went that way. I waited, holding my breath when Clara had stared down the tunnel toward her lost kingdom. She was drawn to her land just as I knew she would be. I could feel the need rolling through her.

Excellent. I knew exactly what to do with her once I stole her away.

They finally moved down the tunnel leading to the

Land of the Flowers. If I hurried, I could not only capture the princess, but I could exact my revenge on the others at the same time. It would be a delicious victory. Far enough away that they wouldn't notice, I shifted again into the form of man and called on my animal speed to get to the cave where the tunnel let out above ground again.

I opened my senses as wide and far as I could, sensing the animals in the area. Some horses would do, but I didn't feel any nearby at all. There were birds, wild boar who were skittish from being hunted, and a den of gentle foxes. I asked them all if they knew where there were any fellow beasts that would carry a band of weary travelers, and they all told me the same thing.

No large animals were to be found in the fae lands. They'd all been hunted for food. I damned my mother for her lazy short-sightedness. The troubles she'd stirred between the fae had the people starving each other out. Hungry fae, even Sweet and Flower would hunt to feed their families.

No docile animal was safe. The bastards. I supposed my people were lucky the fae hadn't come hunting in the Land of Animals.

I stretched my senses even farther and found a small herd of reindeer at the edge of the Christmas Tree Forest. *I promise no harm will come to you here if you offer your aid to my friends. They are on a great quest and under the protection of my army. That protection will extend to you. I give you my word.*

Only part of that was a lie. I wouldn't let harm come to them. I mentally sent orders to my mice to escort the herd here and gnaw out the eyes of anyone who even looked at them hungrily.

But reindeer weren't suited for riding. What we needed was a sleigh. But it wasn't likely I'd find one out here in the Sugar Fae wilderness. Perhaps I could fashion a basic sledge. Even as fast as I ran, it was unlikely the princess and her Guard were more than an hour or so behind me.

I needed more help. This time I reached toward the icy rivers of the bordering Flower Fae lands. I knew just who to call upon. It didn't take me long to find a family of beavers not far away. *Friends, can you help me. I need wood and your best teeth for carving.*

The mental image of the sleigh I wanted excited the elder of their family and he then sent the call for help to others of their kind. Within minutes a whirlwind of woodpeckers, squirrels, chipmunks, and finally the beavers gathered around a thick deep brown tree. It smelled of chocolate, but the beavers assured me it was true wood. It seemed many of the plants in the borderlands were hybrids of sugar and nature.

I set them at their task, knowing their industriousness would be my saving grace. The greedy fae only gathered and consumed the resources around them, instead of trying to live as one with the land. Animal's culture could only add to their bounty, but they refused to see even shifters as little more than stupid servants or pets.

There was one more task to set my trap. My heart beat against my chest faster in anticipation, even though this was going to fucking hurt. If I hadn't been a weak fool, I would have already used the spell.

My weakness wasn't of the flesh, but of the heart. No matter the betrayal, the deep inside, I still believed that the rebellion could defeat the Mouse Queen. I was stupid. They couldn't.

I had to let that dream go.

At the entrance to the cave, I found an arrowhead left from some Flower Fae spy and grabbed it up. It would make a perfect carving tool of my own. In six places, the points of the Christmas Star, I carved the symbol for the Land of Animals into the stone. It was the same mark I wore on my own heart. The one my mother had carved into me the day she discovered I'd joined the Nutcracker Guard in their rebellion.

When the final emblem was carved, I tossed the dulled arrowhead aside, and drew my sword from the scabbard. Before I could think too much about the pain, I was about to inflict on myself, I grabbed the tip of blade in my fist and drove it into my chest.

Fucking hell that hurt. The cold blade burned as it sliced through my skin and muscle. My enhanced shifter healing wouldn't take long to heal me, but that didn't mean I liked the pain in the first place. I pushed the blade in even further until it slipped past my sternum on the right and pierced my heart.

I dropped to my knees and had to grit my teeth not to cry out. Finally, the blade hit the metal of the crown inside and repelled it back out of the wound. The magic of the Land of Animals seeped from my chest along with my blood. I needed that magic, yes, but what I needed more was the curse mixed with it that compelled me to follow the Mouse Queen's commands.

I swiped my fingers through the blood and scrabbled to my feet, lumbering over to the marks I'd carved on the walls. The blood I smeared across the carvings seeped in, sealing the magic and the curse in with it. The moment the crowns she wore on the chain around her neck reached out to find the crown they thought was buried in the stone, just a touch of the curse I carried would be Clara's as well.

She would be compelled to follow my commands.

I spoke the words aloud, groaning them out. "The sleigh is safe, and it will save you time. Use it to find the Sweet Fae crown. Then bring it to me."

My curse was set into motion. I stumbled back out into the light and over to where my animal friends were working. They'd done so much better than I ever could have imagined myself. The reindeer had arrived and the mice with them had used the local grass to tightly weave cushions, blankets, and even a full set of reins.

thank you, my friends. We will be ever grateful, and I am in your service. With that I sent them all back to their homes and found a place among the rocks to hide and wait for Clara and the Nutcrackers.

Tonight, she would be mine.

A STOLEN PRINCESS

CLARA

*T*he pull to walk down the dark passage, toward the place that I was born, yanked at my heart. I didn't remember anything about it. I didn't even realize until this moment that I had even been there before. Up until this very moment, I'd been under the assumption this was my first time in the Winter Realm.

That wasn't correct. This place was my home and something long ago had happened to steal me away from it.

I wanted to know when, why, how, and who'd done this to me. Right off the top of my head, I could think of three people who might know and none of them were standing here with me. Sure, my men probably had some insights and perhaps there were even stories, but they'd been babies when it had all happened too. They'd called me a lost princess, but I wasn't.

I was stolen.

As much as I wanted answers and to see what remained of my birthplace, Tau was right. The best way to get all the answers I wanted to the litany of questions that kept coming up each day I spent here, was to find those crowns.

I touched the symbol Tau had carved into the stone and engraved it on my heart. Somewhere deep inside, a new bit if magic unlocked and I could feel the spirit and magic inside of Leb, Nuss, Zucker, and Tau mixing with mine.

And one other.

We'd been running from the dark warrior, the Mouse Prince Konig, since my arrival, but I felt him in my heart just as I did the others. Someday soon, I needed to run toward him, not away.

In the sparkle of magic where I could feel their spirits, there was love, loyalty, determination, and a deep sense of responsibility. But there was also a sense of loss and betrayal. Those were old wounds, and they weren't healed.

I took one last look into the dark and then stepped over to the passageway marked with the flower. "How far is it?"

Zucker moved into the tunnel, illuminating it with his beautiful purple inner light. "The tunnels all connect to one of the many sugar caves dotting our land. Each are about an hour's walk from the castle.

I had the stamina of a dancer who'd trained hard for years. Just because I had thick thighs, didn't mean I couldn't run. "If we hustle, we could probably make it, what, twenty minutes?"

The need to get this quest to fruition banged against the inside of my chest. Not only because of my want of the truth of what happened to me, but because with each passing moment, the craving to bond with each of my Nutcracker guards grew stronger. I could literally feel the magic in my spirit awakening, stretching, and wanting to reclaim everything I'd missed experiencing here in the Winter Realm. Falling in love, bonding, and consummating that bond were all at the top of my list.

I hoped these ballet slippers held up longer than a couple of performances because running in them would be as hard on them as the leading role in Swan Lake. I started off down the tunnel at a good jog. The men all followed along, and the further we went, the more distinctly I got the feeling I'd been here before.

"Princess, slow down here." Zucker matched my pace and drew his daggers from his belt. "The incline will go up in a moment and we will rise into the cave. There could be any number of enemies waiting for us there."

I was ready for a breather anyway. "Is this the cave you all saw in my dance?"

Tau shook his head. "No, we still need to journey to the border. We could camp in the cave tonight, but I'd rather we continue on now before anyone has a chance to catch up to us. We have the advantage right now since only the Sweet Fae at the party have seen the dance. But news will spread fast."

"I want to keep going. The sooner we find the crown, the better."

Leb drew his axe. "Let me go first. I am enemy only to the mouse army. If there are Flower Fae waiting for us, I'll just knock them down with a stiff blow of Kuchenir."

"Did you name you axe?" Zucker huffed out a laugh.

"Yes. Of course." Leb patted the axe against his huge fist. "You should always give your best weapon a name of reverence. Have I taught you nothing?"

We all stepped aside and let Leb pass, but I looked over at Zucker and Tau. "I want a history of the Fae and their problems later. I thought we'd been helping an already united people against the Mouse Queen, but it seems like you all fight more than Fritz and I do."

Nuss snorted and I pointed at him. "Don't think you're getting away without letting me see into the ooey gooey center of Snowflake culture and whatever happened between you and the Mouse Prince."

If the five of us were going to be bonded, they had

to be a whole lot more open with me and that was starting tonight.

I followed Leb up the slope at a few paces behind because if anyone could just shove some attackers aside, it was my Gingerbread Viking. I imagined most any assassin would pee their pants at the thought of going up against him.

Zucker had said these were sugar caves and I'd imagined they'd be filled with crystals of sugar sort of like the salt caves back home. The miners in the salt mines of Salzburg had even carved intricate designs and even statues into the stone and salt. We found the cave empty except for the dazzling crystals. Perhaps that was a small, but nice bit of human culture to add to all the amazing things I'd learned about in the Winter Realm.

"Let's keep moving, I can practically feel the crown calling to me." I hurried to forward through the cave, heading toward the new bit of light from the outside.

It wasn't long before moonlight joined the auras of Zucker and Tau. Leb took the lead again and was the first out of the cavern. After so much darkness, even with the purple and green light of my Fae men's inner lights, the reflection of the moon off the snow outside was glaring.

I looked away, and if I hadn't, I would have missed the symbol freshly carved into the rock at the very entrance to the cave. I'd seen the very same one at the intersection of the tunnels that represented the one that went toward the Land of Animals. A mouse wearing a crown.

Konig was here. Or he had been. Recently.

I quickly made myself look anywhere but the symbol. I absolutely knew that I should tell everyone what I'd seen. But I didn't.

"The coast is clear," Leb shouted from outside. "And someone has left us a present."

We rushed outside and found him standing, arms wide, in the back of a pale blue sleigh, decorated with an intricate snowflake motif, hooked up to eight reindeer. Nuss cracked a grin and walked over to the closest animal and patted it on the back, then ran his hand along its neck, expertly ducked under the rack of antlers, and adjusted the harness. "Now this is my kind of ride. Where did you come from, you beauties?"

The animal responded with a snort and a snuffle of Nuss's hand. "Oh, ho. I don't have any treats for you, but I promise to find you something sweet when we reach our destination."

Aww. I hadn't seen Nuss this animated since the first moment I met him under my Christmas tree. He had an adorably soft spot for animals and someday, I was going to get him a puppy just to see his reaction.

"These guys will get us where we need to go quickly." Nuss bounded back to us and jumped into the front and took the reins in his good hand. He looked at me, Zucker, and Tau with a hurry-up face.

"Are we not questioning whose sleigh this is or who

left it for us? This is pretty damn suspicious." Zucker crossed his arms and Tau didn't move.

Nuss smiled and shook his head. "If they've been used nefariously, they'd know and be fidgety. I don't know how they got here, and we may be stealing someone's ride, but we are within walking distance of the castle and they can get there safely."

He was the last one I expected to be so trusting. I had a sneaking suspicion where these animals had come from.

"Princess," Nuss's voice was on the verge of pleading. He held out his hand to me. "Open your spirit to these animals. You may be able to sense something about them."

"I've never done something like that. You know more about my magic than I do. Can you help me?" I wasn't really looking forward to him cutting me like he had Fritz, but I also wanted to know if my guess was right. I touched my lips briefly thinking about the biting kiss he'd given me and then shook my head. No way. That had been in the moment, and he wouldn't do that again.

Nuss's entire countenance changed, and he was back to the wary man he'd been the past two days. He handed the reins back to Leb and climbed back down. In three quick strides, he was right in front of me. I held out my wrist thinking that would be the easiest place for him to nick my skin. He didn't even look down to my proffered hand. He hauled me into his arm, bent me back, like I'd seen in the movies, and kissed the magic right out of me.

This was no chaste kiss, there was no reticence, but it also wasn't hurried and flurried like during the avalanche. Nuss kissed me with pure wanton need and lust, and I was here for it. My magic swirled between us, sparkling behind my eyelids, and tickling the edges of the connection between me and everyone else here.

Including Konig.

I gasped and Nuss broke away from me, although he didn't let me up. "What do you see, princess of my heart?"

I blinked up at him and not only saw Nuss, but a blue aura all around him. He stood me back up and the entire world around us had the same blue glow as he did. I quickly searched for Konig but couldn't see anyone else. Yet, I knew he was there, but only my sense of his spirit told me so.

"I don't entirely understand what I'm seeing. It's like the magic from when we bonded, but it's everywhere, around every living thing." I blinked my eyes, thinking the blue haze might fade, but it continued so strong it was if I could reach out and touch it.

"That's spirit, allowing you to see it." Nuss nodded toward the animals and then motioned to the each of the men. "All living things have it, but only those who can control magic can see it."

Nuss's blue spirit glow sparkled with hundreds of tiny white lights, like falling snow. Except in a sort of cross over his heart, and his broken arm. They were both dark as if in a shadow. Leb's spirit was dotted with oranges and golds and had a few darker areas around his hands. Tau's was lined in the same green of his aura, but he too had dark spots, but his were across his forehead. Zucker's spirit was laced with purple, and the darkness from him was right across his chest.

I think I was seeing wounds of their spirit. When I looked at the animals and plants around us, their spirits were solid and glowing bright with all the colors of the natural world. "I don't see any darkness around the reindeer at all. They seem happy and healthy if the pretty glow of their spirits is anything to go by."

"That's exactly as I thought. This sleigh hasn't been placed here nefariously, but perhaps by the Christmas Star herself to help us fulfill her quest." Nuss grabbed my hand and guided me up into the sleigh.

I waited until all five of us were seated before I finally let the truth out. I couldn't and wouldn't keep secrets from them and it had been a stupid decision to think I ever should. "I don't think it was the Christmas Star who left this for us. It was Konig."

All four of them stood back up and drew their weapons. They held them out, pointing in every which direction looking for an enemy. I sighed and rubbed my head.

"He's not here now. Or I didn't see him or his spirit anyway. I don't know the history between you all and him, but this is the second time he's helped us to get away from the Mouse Army, so I think we should trust him a little bit. Enough to take the sleigh and go get that piece of the broken crowns."

Not a one of them responded. They were all on high alert and protecting me apparently meant ignoring me all of a sudden.

The intensity of the glow of the spirit all around me was fading, except for one bright and golden glow just over the next hill. "The crown is waiting for us. I can see its spirit too."

Nope. Still nothing. I wasn't used to them ignoring me. Funny how I had been used to that everyone in my old life in the human world, but not at all since I'd met the four of them. What happened to earlier today when I was the warrior general? I was only getting stronger, but suddenly, they were treating me like a fragile porcelain doll.

Fine. I'd take matters into my own hands. I picked up the reins that Nuss had dropped and gave them a little flick. A burst of my magic went through them, and the animals surged forward. The men all fell back into the seats as we took off across the snow and I giggled my butt off.

There was more than one way to end a conversation and remind them that I was stronger than they thought. I'm sure I'd hear all about it when we reached our destination, and they'd all be on high alert, but I just had this gut feeling deep inside that reuniting them with Konig was going to be important and would be good for them all.

That was the first time I'd accessed any of my magic on my own. I wasn't entirely sure how I'd done it, but when I needed it, there it was. If loving on my men was the best way to access it, I wasn't going to be sad about that even a little bit. I'd rather that than have to sacrifice some blood. The idea of kissing and making love and sharing a bonding experience being the key to the magic settled in nicely in my psyche next to my mission to bring love back to the Winter Realm.

Everything I'd learned today made it even more clear that all the lands needed more love and a whole lot less hate. Hate was exhausting. No wonder they were all fighting all the time.

I looked around at each of my protectors to make sure they weren't too upset with me. They were. Nuss grumped and held out his hands for the reins. I was going to tell him that I had this, but then remembered the affection he'd had for the reindeer. I didn't need to prove I was a strong woman, not with him, not with any of them.

I placed the strips of leather into his hand and snugged up against him, threading my arm through his bandaged one. Someday I would learn how to use my magic to heal both his physical and spiritual wound. Perhaps when he and I bonded.

The Land of Snowflakes was definitely next on my list. Leb, Zucker, and Tau kept their weapons at the ready, but we made quick time in the sleigh. It was almost as if the crown was pulling us to it, that it was waiting to be found.

In fact, as we got closer to the shining light of spirit at our destination there was much more waiting for us than just the Sweet Fae's broken piece of the seven crowns.

THE GROTTO OF LOVE

CLARA

*T*au tapped Nuss on the shoulder as we got close to the cave where the broken piece of the Sweet Fae crown was hidden. He pointed to the enormous trees on the far side of the cave entrance. They reminded me of those long tree-lined walkways with branches draped in long flowy moss. But these ones had mounds of pink fluff hanging down from the canopy above, and the air was scented with both the woodsy scent of a forest and the sweetness of cotton candy.

Most of my spirit vision had faded, but I could still make out the green auras of at least half a dozen Flower Fae hiding in the branches. The men stiffened and I wasn't surprised that as warriors they'd spotted the ambush too. Tau spoke so only the four of us could hear him. "They won't shoot as long as I'm with you and they think I am unharmed. I suggest you allow me to go into the cave with you first, Princess."

"I know that I don't understand all the politics of what's going on here, but I'd like to make a statement by walking in with both you at my side."

Tau glanced to Zucker, and they did that communication with their eyes that only someone with their close connection can. Zucker nodded and the three of us got out of the sleigh. Leb and Nuss stayed, looking slightly awkward and not knowing what to do with themselves.

"I've changed my mind," I said. If I was going to make a statement, might as well go big. "I want all four of you with me, as a united front. Let your kinsman see that I play no favorites and hold no alliance or bond over any other. You are all important to me and I could do none of this without each one of you."

Leb gave me a big old grin and hopped out of the sleigh. "I'd kiss you, lass, if I wasn't sure I'd get an arrow in the back for it."

There was the tiniest bit of vulnerability in Leb's tone. I'd assumed he and I were solid now that we were bonded, but I needed to remember this relationship was just as new to the four of them as it was to me. They might have grown up on stories of our connection and pledged themselves to be my guard, my protectors, but none of us had had more than half a day where we weren't fighting or running to even get to know each other or express our feelings.

"I'd kiss you back, my ginger giant." I blew him a kiss anyway.

Nuss remained in the sleigh. "What about Konig and the mouse army?"

In my mind I included Konig as one of my men. I wasn't sure of what his role in this battle between good and evil I'd drop in on, but in my heart, I knew he was on my side. "If he shows up, we'll deal with that then."

I don't think Nuss liked that answer. I was starting to understand that he was the kind of guy that needed a plan, with a contingency plan, and probably a back-up plan for that. But the next few days were probably going to be pretty harried, and we were going to have to be adaptable. I wanted to wrap him up in a big hug and tell him this was going to work out.

I didn't know that it was, but I was going to believe it.

Nuss had been the stalwart captain all this time, my hero from minute one. His reticence was new to me. I wished I understood him better. Land of Snowflakes, I was coming for you next because I'll be damned if I'd allow him to feel anything less than as strong and powerful as the Nutcracker Captain I know he'd trained to be.

I walked back to the sleigh and took his hand.

"Believe, captain. Believe in me, believe in us, believe in the magic. Everything will be okay."

A spark of my magic zipped from my hand to his and the soldier who'd come for me under the Christmas tree was back in his eyes. "You might be the only thing I believe in, Princess Clara."

He jumped from the sleigh and the two of us joined the rest of my guard. The four of them formed a box around me, Tau and Nuss in front, Zucker and Leb at my back. We moved forward as a unit and into the entrance of the cave.

It took a moment for my eyes to adjust, because it was both dark, and brilliantly lit from the spirit light of the broken crown... or should I say, crowns. I could see now that there were two lights, one lined in green, the other laced with purple. But they weren't two separate lights, all three colors were intertwined.

I blinked a few times, and the rest of the cave came into focus. Like the sugar cave we were in before there were giant crystals all along the walls, but where those ones had been clear and white, these were every color of the rainbow. "Whoa, no wonder the Vivandiere chose this place to hide the crowns. The atmosphere around is befitting their magic."

"I've been to this cave before," Tau said, as much wonder in his voice as I felt. "It didn't look like this at all. Come on let's go in deeper to where the flowers grow."

"Underground flowers? How do they grow with no light?"

Tau laughed. "Wait until you see this. The sugar crystals reflect light down into the cavern below. Right where our two land's border there is an underground grotto, filled with the most beautiful flora and fauna."

"How many times have you been here?" Zucker asked Tau. It is a bit of edge to his voice that I hadn't heard between them before. I didn't like that. The sooner we found the crowns the better.

"Only once in my youth. It's forbidden for all but the royal DewDrop Court. And even then, only on incredibly special occasions. My father brought me the night before my archer's test. He said he wanted to show me what we fought for."

"If we had met serving in the nutcracker guard, what do you have fought me for this treasure?"

Tau froze in his tracks. He turned and grabbed the back of Zucker's neck in the same way I'd seen Zucker do to him. "I think once you'll see it, you'll understand. I've never been able to get this place out of my mind, and it is the reason, along with the prophecy and the princess, that I did join the nutcracker guard. Places like this shouldn't be only for the privileged. I want this to be for the whole realm."

The connection between the two of them zipped through me as well. This time the magic was not just all awe-inspiring, but sensual. Those zings went down my spine and settled between my legs. The love between them made me want them even more.

Leb leaned down and whispered in my ear. "You will be the stuff of my pure fantasies when you bond with the two of them. I can hardly wait."

I'd never been anyone's fantasy before. It seemed silly but those naughty words gave me even more confidence than Leb's warrior magic or feeling like a warrior woman myself. Perhaps because I could see myself commanding troops if I had to. Even under Fritz's thumb, I'd always done what I had to do to keep our family going.

I'd never seen myself as a sexual being. Not until last night when he and I consummated our bond. But that experience was so new and unique that I hadn't thought about what it would feel like to do it all over again with each of my men. Of course, I knew I'd bond with each of them, and consummating that bond meant sex, but I guess I hadn't actually thought about it in that way. I'd been so focused on showing their world how to love again, I forgot, I was the one who would be falling in love.

Somehow... that also meant falling in love with myself. As a warrior woman, as a princess, as a dancer, and as a lover— a sexual being in my own right.

I felt the heat of a blush creep up my cheeks before I even said what I was thinking to Leb, but I said it anyway. "I can hardly wait for you to watch."

I refused to think I was weird for liking it when Nuss watched, and I would enjoy it just as much when Leb did too. Although now I was wondering what it would be like when none of them were watching, and we were all entangled together.

Leb kissed me on the top of my head and then gave me a swat on the butt, moving us along the path. The deeper we went into the cavern, the warmer it got. For being the Winter Realm, it was downright tropical in this cave. I pulled at the tight bodice on the ballerina's costume I still wore and longed a tank top and shorts.

Tau and Zucker rushed ahead and the three of us simply followed the path that was indeed lit up by the reflection from crystal to crystal. Interestingly, the spirit light from the crowns didn't bounce off the chunks of sugar in the walls. It wasn't really light then, was it? Another kind of magic, I supposed.

While I'd learned so much about the magic inside of me, I wondered if there would ever be anyone from the Land of Spirit and Magic who could teach me about my innate abilities like there had been someone for each of my men.

When I caught up to Zucker and Tau, they were standing together, hand in hand looking out over an underground oasis. Colorful crystals hung not only from the walls, but from vines, trees, and flowers. Bees and butterflies flew from bud to bud, and the air sparkled with a hundred thousand fireflies.

I came up beside them and found what they were staring at. In the center of the pool, there was a small grassy island and growing straight up from the center of it was an enormous dewdrop flower, with its pastel green and violet petals open wide. While the giant flower was spectacular, it was the fact that the stem was wrapped in a vine of candy canes. The two were so intertwined that every inch of the flower itself sparkled with fine sugar crystals. At the tip of each of the thin filaments of the stamen, instead of a typical anther pod, I could swear was a sugar plum sweet.

I turned around and faced my two Fae princes and touched my palms to each of their cheeks. "That's where we'll find the broken pieces of the crowns, from both the Sweet and Flower Fae lands."

Leb clapped them both on the back. "As it should be, lads. Now let's go get it. Anyone know how to swim?"

Oh. Ha. I hadn't thought of that. I didn't suppose there was a whole lot of swimming in a land where everything was ice and snow. "I can."

I hated to get my clothes wet if we were going back out into the frosty winter. I guess I'd have to take them off. But I hadn't even put them on myself. I wasn't sure I could get out of them on my own. I undid the ribbons on the shoes and slipped them off, but I'd need help with everything else.

"Can you help me get out of this bodice? I don't want to swim in this outfit and get my clothes wet."

Tau, Zucker, and Leb all reached for me with a sparkle in their eyes, but Nuss batted their hands away.

"Allow me."

I scoffed at him. "I can undress myself, thank you very much."

"Let me do this, princess." Nuss's tone had gone back to the captain of the guard, man in charge, delicious kisser and I melted.

He turned me so I faced the pool and had my back to all of them. I felt the bodice's lacings tug and then loosen bit by bit. It had never been tight and uncomfortable before, but now I found that I couldn't breathe. I waited for his fingers to touch my skin, to send that flash of magic to caress the connection between us. All I felt was Nuss's breath on the back of my neck. He was so close yet said nothing until the top was loose enough to take off.

"Lift your arms over your head." I did as he told and the anticipation of having his fingers brush over me as he pulled it off was killing me.

Zucker and Tau stepped to my sides, and each grabbed the hem. They skimmed it up and off, leaving me naked from the waist up. I dropped my hands to cover my bare breasts and waited. Was Nuss finished with me so soon?

But no. My Fae Princes moved away and Nuss pressed himself to my back. He wrapped his arm around my waist and found the tiny ribbons securing the fluffy skirt at my waist. With a flick of his wrist, the ties were undone, and he pushed his hand down into space between the material and my stomach.

I sucked in a long, deep gasp as his hand continued down much farther and he cupped my pussy. "Never think that I don't want to share in giving you pleasure. Everything I am and have is for you."

"But?" I could hear it coming in his intonation, so I pushed him to continue.

"You need to have time to bond with each member of your guard. I will give you that, because when it's my turn, when we have the Snowflake crown in hand, I'm not going to want to share this, share you."

I opened and closed my mouth, the words being blocked by the pure lust his declaration had bubbling up inside of me. I'd always thought I'd ever only be with one man. Now I couldn't imagine not being with all my men. So, I didn't understand why Nuss's possessiveness was sending tingles through my core. "But I thought you agreed to the kind of bonding the Gingerbread Kingdom has with their women."

He pressed his lips to my ear and stroked over the soft fabric covering my pussy. "I have, and I will share your magic, your love, and your body with each of my brethren, but when you and I consummate our bond, you will be mine and mine alone for that one brief moment."

Before I could respond to his words, he shoved the skirt down my legs to pool at my feet. He followed it down, coming around and kneeling in front of me. "Leb, come and get her skirt."

Leb came over and waggled his eyebrows at me but didn't say a word. I'd needed him to break this tension, and he left me to the wolves, or rather the puppy who'd turned into a wolf before me.

Nuss took my hand and set it against one hip, then placed his own on the other. "Push the tights down for me."

He wasn't asking, and I was sure as sugar complying. The tights and soft panties underneath inched down my thighs, a little on my side, a bit on his, until they were at my knees and my pussy was bared to him. He stared at me and licked his lips, and I felt the wetness build between my legs. Would he taste me, right here, right now in front of the others?

With a final nudge, the tights and panties dropped past my knees, and I stepped out of them. Nuss plucked the panties out of the pile and stuck them into the pocket of his jacket. "When you consummate your bonds tonight, I'll be watching again, and stroking my cock with these."

Whoo, man. I swallowed and pulled my bottom lip between my teeth. He had me more than ready. And I'd thought Zucker was the master of sensuality and anticipation.

Nuss stood and stepped aside. Zucker and Tau came up and escorted me down the short slope until the water of the grotto's pool tickled my toes. I dipped one foot in, and it felt funny until I realized the water was exactly the same temperature as my body.

"You're sure you're safe swimming to the flower's island?" Tau let go of my fingers as I walked in deeper.

"I'm sure. Unless there are any marshmallow crocodiles or strawberry stinging jelly-fish."

I probably shouldn't have said that.

LOVE IS LOVE IS LOVE

ZUCKER

I'd never known real fear until I watched Clara glide silently through the water in this strange underground grotto. To watch her strong athletic movements propel her so easily from this sugar crystal shoreline and across the invisible border between the Land of Sweets and the Land of Flowers had my own heart pounding.

I was normally an enthusiastic fan of the trembling of my very cells in anticipation but seeing her go to a place that I couldn't, had me fidgety and feeling help-less. I paced at the water's edge. What the fuck were we going to do if something went wrong while she was in the water? Go out there and drown ourselves?

I was ready to crawl out of my skin, much less my

clothes. "Tau, the Land of Flowers is filled with rivers and lakes, surely you've learned to swim in them."

He shook his head. His arms wrapped around him projected just how nervous he was too. Likely feeding off my emotions. "They're freezing. More than a moment in them and its death. I've never seen a body of water this warm."

"The lake in the Land of Spirit and Magic is warm," Nuss said like that wasn't the news of the century.

"How do you know that?" Leb asked. He was the calmest of us all. Perhaps because he was bonded with Clara and saw her as a powerful warrior woman like all the Gingerbread Vikings.

The Land of Snowflakes bordered what used to be Princess Clara's land, but there was nothing more there now than a darkness that would steal anyone's spirit who even approached it. Or so we'd all heard.

Nuss sighed.

"Don't keep secrets from us now, captain asshole." Leb smacked him on the back hard enough to make him stumble forward to the water's edge.

Nuss caught himself just before his boots hit the water. "There's a lot about the Snowflake Court and the Church of the Christmas Star that you don't know."

I thought we were a tight unit. We'd all made a commitment to each other and to Clara. This was all too much like when Konig betrayed us. We'd never been the same since, but we'd made it work. "Like how you're able access Clara and Friedrich's magic?"

"Yes."

"Why are we finding out about this now?" This nervous energy inside me had to get out and if I couldn't use it to keep Clara safe, I was just as happy picking a fight.

Until Clara screamed.

Luckily my training as an elite Nutcracker guard meant I knew how to fight even when my own heart wasn't beating in my chest. I walked straight into the water, but Leb grabbed me from behind and dragged me back to shore. "Look, she's alright."

Clara bobbed in the water and held her arm up, holding some kind of green stringy plant. "Sorry. I'm okay. It's just that this brushed up against my legs. Umm, it's seaweed, I guess? It smells like green apple saltwater taffy."

She took a small nibble out of it and nodded. "Yep. This is such a strange place."

Her laughter was the only thing that restarted my blood pumping through my veins. Tau put his hand on my shoulder and squeezed. "First thing after this war is over, we're all learning to swim."

It wasn't another moment before Clara reached the island and climbed up on its shores. As she approached the flower, hundreds of smaller buds bloomed at her feet, forming a path around her. She was a nature goddess come to life before our eyes.

"I found them." She reached up to the large candy cane and dewdrop blossom, and I swear it bent to her.

The most powerful scent of violets, plums, and peppermint wafted to us, and it acted like an aphrodisiac. My cock went instantly hard, and Tau moaned beside me.

Which piece of the broken crown has she found? I wanted so badly for it to be the Land of Sweets so I could claim her body for my own. But equally needed it to be the Land of Flowers so I could see her and Tau together.

Clara reached up and plucked something from the center of the flower and held it to her chest. Magic like I'd never felt before exploded into the grotto and both Tau and I were yanked from the shore dragged across the water to the island. We tumbled into the soft flowers around her, and she let out an excited laugh.

"Look." She held out the item she plucked from the flower and in her hand were two broken pieces of the seven crowns. The Flower Fae crown with its green and bendy vines that had grown around the purple sparkling sugary crown of the Sweet Fae.

"No wonder you two are so close. The spirits of your people are so intertwined, they can't be separated." She knelt in the flowers in front of us and bent her head. "Help me take the necklace off so I can join them with the other two."

I unclipped the fastening on the chain and the crowns from the Land of Spirit and Magic she'd brought with her from the human realm, and the one Mother Gingerbread had given her from the Gingerbread Kingdom fell into her waiting hands.

She slipped the chain through the vines of the Flower Fae crown right where it met the stylized Sugar Plum of the Sweet Fae crown. Then she put the necklace back on letting all four crowns dangle between her breasts. Her eyes rolled back in her head, and she let out a sighed whimper that had both Tau and I rushing to take off our clothes.

"I need you both, right now." A flush rose up Clara's breasts and her eyes went dark with lust. "Is this the effect of finding the crowns?"

Clara reached for my shirt and tried to pull it over my head, but it was a struggle since I was doing the same to Tau.

"Only you and Leb can answer that," I said and just ripped Tau's shirt open.

Leb's laugh boomed across the water. He cupped his hands and shouted to us, "Yes, it is."

Tau pushed Clara's hands away and tore my shirt open as well. "I've never felt so frantic to be with anyone like this in my life. I need to be with you, both and it feels like I'll die if I don't."

Clara was already naked, and I ran my hands down her arms and across her chest, teasing her with my touch, while avoiding her breasts. She leaned forward into me, and her hard little nipples pushed against my flesh, sending a shockwave of magic through me that turned to pure sexuality.

Tau pushed himself up against her back, so she was between us and grabbed her hands, directing them down to unbuckle my belt. They worked together and I did my best to distract them both with kisses and nips to Clara's throat, ear, and finally her lips.

I kissed her like I'd never get enough of her. There was so much more to this kiss than any I'd stolen from her before. It was as if I'd never experienced touching my mouth and tongue to someone else's before. The flavor of her exploded across my tastebuds and every emotion, want, and need I had was amplified times a thousand.

"Stars, I can literally feel what you're each experiencing as if I'm the one kissing her and you and the same time." Tau's voice filtered in low and husky and needy.

Their fingers finally released the fastenings to my pants, and I couldn't get them over my hips fast enough. I wanted both their hands on me now. I felt Tau's fist wrap around my cock first and then he guided Clara's softer hand to do the same just above his. Together they stroked up so slowly, I was sure to perish before her fingers squeezed the head and then went back down again before I was ready.

"He's this hard for you, sweet flower. You're going to love having this big cock inside of you, Zucker pounding into your cunt, making you cry out his name."

Clara groaned and shivered with each of my kisses. "Yes, I want that."

I dragged myself away from their touch. My need

for them both was greater than any arousal I'd ever felt, but I was no inexperienced selfish lover. They too would know pleasure at my hands. Frantic, frenzied fucking was fun, sure. Consummating a bond with one's true north should be more sacred than this.

I had to be the one to control the scene and give them both a delirious number of orgasms if I was to prove myself as deserving of being their partner in love and life. "If you keep stroking me like that, we won't get to the pounding part."

Tau and I had been lucky enough to be a part of her first sexual experience bonding with Leb. We needed to make this one just as special for her. I also recognized this was a unique experience for me and Tau. We always knew we'd each be bonding with the princess, but he'd been right when he'd said it would bring us closer together.

Our lives were as intertwined as the crowns Clara had found, now our spirits could be too. I had to hope this was the missing piece he'd felt between us. That tonight as we bonded with Clara, that our own bond would be consummated as well. Because I was nothing without him.

Suddenly, I knew how to make this bonding perfect and right for all three of us. To make it work, we needed Clara's body to be supple, relaxed, and her cunt as wet as possible. Stars, I was going to love getting her body ready, and pushing Tau's to the edge.

"Stay on your knees, sweet princess, but spread

your legs nice and wide. Tau and I are going to get you make you come so you're wet and ready to take our cocks. Together."

That delicious pink flush raced up her chest to her throat and cheeks. "Both of you at the same time?"

Behind her Tau's eyes went dark and sparkling. My sexual prowess and his empathic gift were saturated in Clara's magic, and I had no doubt he got every single mental image I had of the two of us taking her simultaneously. He helped steady her as I pushed her legs open and then quickly shucked his own pants.

He was normally much better with words than I was, but there was something in the way his muscles were tensed, and his breathing already rapid that told me he was feeling overwhelmed. We certainly hadn't expected to find the Flower Fae crown tonight. None of us thought all three of us would be consummating our bonds on only this second day of Christmas.

This was so damn important to him. More than I'd ever understood before. There was one gift that I could give to him in our joint bonding with Clara.

"Yes, at the same time." But Tau was going to get take her body, slide his cock into her cunt first. It would mean everything to him to have that one moment where she belonged only to him. It wasn't as important to me as having them both be mine.

I laid flat on my back and shimmied to put my face between her spread legs. It certainly wasn't going to take much to get her ready. Her thighs were already glistening wet. I licked the inside of one thigh and then the other. I could taste the sweetness of the sugary water she'd had to swim though to get here on her skin. "Lean forward, down on your hands and knees. I'm going to suck on your luscious clit while Tau stretches your cunt with his fingers to prepare you for our cocks."

I didn't wait for her to get herself settled before I dragged her hips down and ran my tongue up through her pussy lips. She was as sweet as anything I'd ever put in my mouth before. Clara sank down onto my face and I loved that she wasn't shy about taking her pleasure from me.

I gave her a good couple of flicks of her clit before I sucked it into her into my mouth.

"Oh my God," she moaned and more of her juices coated my lips and jaw. She was so close already, and I was just getting started. Her little bud fluttered in my mouth. If she came so quickly, I was going to start counting how many times she climaxed just to see how many we could ring out of her.

While my face was buried in her luscious cunt, I felt Tau crawl over me, straddling my chest and he came up behind Clara. "Bend down, as you're told, sweet flower, or you'll get a spanking instead of my fingers in your cunt."

That had her getting even more wet. As Leb had proven last night, she was turned on by a little bite of pain with her pleasure. I'd remember that for later.

Apparently, Tau hadn't forgotten and as he bent Clara over me, he gave her a slap to the ass anyway. She gasped and I kept lapping and suckling at her quivering cunt. I pulled away for just a moment. "She likes that, Tau. Do it again."

I didn't wait for him to do it before I dived back in, because if a spanking was going to get her to come, I wanted every bit of that magic in my mouth.

Tau spanked her three times and then pushed two of his fingers into her cunt. I gave them a quick lick to let him know what was in store for later.

"Oh, oh. How do your fingers feel just as big as Leb's whole cock inside of me?" Her head dropped and her hair flicked over my waist, the strands tickling my own member.

As if I wasn't already hard as a fucking candy cane, my cock stood up straighter, got even stiffer, and the first drops of my seed leaked from the tip knowing her mouth was this close. My hips jerked of their own accord just wanting to feel the warmth of her breath.

"You're so fucking tight. Relax, sweet flower or we'll never be able to get inside of you." Tau's fingers went in and out of her slick cunt and I lapped at them both.

The only thing better than this would be if it was his cock sliding across my tongue and into her cunt. To my dismay, Tau withdrew and yanked Clara upright. I continued to eat her sweet pussy and waited for whatever it was he was preparing to do. I trusted him completely with her body and mine.

Tau whispered something to Clara, and he must have said exactly the right thing to her because her legs clenched tighter around my head and her thighs trembled. Come on, baby let me taste that orgasm.

She bent back over me, and I thought I was prepared for anything and everything. Nothing in this realm or the next had me ready to feel Clara's mouth wrap around my cock head and suckle while Tau's dick slid into her cunt right in front of my eyes.

The magic between the three of us connected in a way it hadn't before as if a missing piece of a puzzle had just locked into place and that puzzle was a map of love, life, and the answer to all the mysteries of the universe all in one.

Not only could I feel their bodies, but I sensed how they each felt as I touched them. The sensation of me licking Clara's clit mixed with the sensations of Tau's cock pumping in and out of her, and the utter bliss of her tongue swirling around the sensitive underside of my cock head. I was living the reality of every touch, taste, sight, smell, and sound they experienced along with my own.

It was more than I'd ever imagined, and I would never get enough.

ROMANCE IS THE LANGUAGE OF BELONGING

TAU

I'd been searching my whole life for a connection that I was never sure I'd ever find. The first time Zucker kissed me, I felt so close to touching that thing I needed, I'd almost come in my pants. The first time he fucked me, I was sure we'd find it together.

But there was always something missing, a bit of magic just out of reach. I loved Zucker like I'd never loved anyone, more than I even thought possible, and I hated that it wasn't enough.

At first, as we trained, and then discovered the other Princes born under the Christmas star, then formed an alliance among ourselves to find the lost princess, I told myself it didn't matter. But the nearer we got to finding a way through the Christmas Tree portal, the more anxious I felt.

No matter how many times Zucker and I fucked each other, I was never fully satisfied. I hid that fact from him because I didn't want him to be hurt. My own spirit was battered and bruised even thinking that he might ever discover my secret.

The night she came to us, I finally knew. She was the missing piece. That must be it. I was destined to love the Princess of Spirit and Magic, and here she was right in front of me. Loving her didn't mean my feelings for Zucker were any less than before, in fact, I was sure it would only make them stronger.

I had no idea, that bonding with her would change everything. I'd thought it would make a new connection, deepen the one I had with Zucker, and even bring me closer to the other Nutcrackers. All I ever wanted was to feel like I belonged to a something bigger than the small, narrow-minded, hateful world of most Flower Fae.

I wanted to belong to my brothers in arms and to the princess, and them to me.

I had a feeling that something special would happen when the three of us were truly joined. I whispered instructions on how to take Zucker into her mouth and use her tongue to make him feel good. I felt the first zip of magic when she did as I told her. The moment I pushed my cock into Clara's tight cunt and the three of us were entwined in a circle of love, life, sex, and bonding, her magic exploded through us and the nirvana running from the two of them to me and back was exhilarating.

Not only was I experiencing everything they did, I could also sense Leb and Nuss. It was as if their two hands were also stroking over my cock along with the tight inner muscles of Clara's pussy.

I glanced over to the shoreline and both Leb and Nuss had their trousers open and their dicks in their hands. I wondered if they could feel this connection too or was it only me and Zucker while we were physically connected Clara.

Perhaps we'd find out when Nuss finally nutted up and joined us in pleasuring our princess.

Clara had been well and truly fucked last night by Leb, so as much as I wanted to fuck her fast and hard, I held myself back, sliding in and out of her wet pussy with a steady rhythm, not pushing her too hard. Zucker wasn't holding back in the least.

He loved having his head between soft, luscious thighs, almost as much as he loved licking a dick. There was power in being able to make someone come that way, and it fueled the innate sexual gift that the Sweet Fae possessed. His power of allure was always strongest after making someone come for him.

I would know.

Clara's inner muscles tightened like a fist opening and squeezing around my cock. With each bob of her head, each of my thrusts into her, and stroke of Leb and Nuss's hand, she was closer and closer to tipping into her first orgasm. It was going to be almost impossible not to come when she did, but I would somehow manage.

I didn't want to spill my seed until Zucker, and I were inside of her together. Our essences mixing together in her cunt, and maybe even her womb. I would swoon over a baby with his purple eyes, her blonde hair, and my green aura. That would be magic indeed.

She moaned deep and lifted her head, arching her back. "It's too much, I can't hold on. Ohh, yes."

Her pussy fluttered around my cock, and I shoved in deep, wanting to give her something to come around and not wanting to miss a moment of her orgasm.

Zucker popped his head out from between her legs and grabbed his cock pumping it fast and hard. "Holy fuck, I can feel her coming as if it's my own climax. Fuck, fuck, Clara, fuck."

He spurted onto his belly and his climax added another layer to the pure bliss surrounding us in its lust-filled haze of magic.

I clenched my own teeth so hard I tasted blood. I'd sacrifice that so as not to come yet. I grabbed the base of my cock and squeezed hard to hold the impending orgasm back. That was a trick he'd taught me when neither of us could get enough of each other's bodies, so we'd wanted to fuck all night. Sweet Fae could come over and over, but I had my limits.

Clara collapsed over Zucker's body, and I slipped from her pussy. The magical connection to everyone's emotions and physical feelings didn't simply break when our bodies were no longer joined. It was more like a slow drain with the connection only fading little by little. Leb and Nuss hadn't come yet, and I could still feel both stroking, getting closer to orgasm themselves.

Wait. Holy fuck, it was three. There were three hands stroking. I distinctly felt a third.

I shot a quick look down to see if Zucker had his hand on his cock again, but both of his were caressing Clara's plump ass. Who else was here in this quiet secluded sanctuary invading our bond?

Just as I was about to sound the alarm, the feeling faded and no matter how far out I tried to reach with my empathic senses juiced up on Clara's magic, I found no other consciousness other than the small creatures who inhabited the grotto.

No one else seemed even the least bit concerned, including Zucker and Clara, whom I knew were feeling everything I was. I must have been mistaken or imagined it with all the intensity of everyone else's experience hitting me at the same time. The last of the magical swirls of our connection finally faded.

I dropped to the ground to join the two of them. "You'd better get your second wind. We're just getting started."

Clara giggled and the sounds was just as magical as her moans during orgasm. I grabbed her and rolled her, so she was on top of me, straddling my waist. I placed her just so and pushed my cock between her folds, rubbing my head across her sensitive clit.

She gasped and threw her head back, rocking her hips and rubbing herself along the length of my hard dick. "You're both still hard, but Tau, did you not reach your climax?"

The pressure of her body pressing down on me as I slid through her pussy lips was as good as pumping into her wet channel. Only this was even better because she was in charge, she was pleasuring herself with my body. "I'm waiting to be inside of you with Zucker."

She looked down at me with those bright sparkling eyes and bit her lip. "I... don't see how you'll both fit."

Zucker rolled to his knees and crawled behind Clara, pushing his way between my knees. He wrapped his arms around Clara and cupped her lovely round tits in his hands. "It will be achingly tight, sweet one, but that's why Tau fucked you, and we made you come first. To open your body and relax your channel."

He bumped his hips against Clara's forcing her to slide her pussy across my dick again and again. I concentrated hard on counting each and every strand of hair on her head to keep my body in check. Zucker knew exactly what he was doing to me. His favorite game to play was to see how far he could push me before I came for him. It was even more fun with Clara between us.

"I want to seal the bond between us, and you two are going to make me spill my seed before I'm ready. Take me into your body again, my flower. I need you, both, now." I grabbed her hips and stopped their slow torture.

Zucker smiled and buried it in the crook of her neck. He whispered to her, but loud enough for me to hear what he said. "I was hoping you'd suck on Tau's cock and taste yourself on him, but I can see he wouldn't last a second in your talented mouth."

Clara batted her eyelashes at me, and stars in the sky, I was in trouble if these two were in league with each other to fuck the living nature out of me. She covered my hands with her own. "If the fates allow, we'll have plenty of time for all of you to teach me every single thing you'd each like best for me to do with your bodies. But I too want to complete the bond. We were so close to something new and special before that I think together, we can make magic."

Make magic, make love, make life.

Zucker nodded in a way that was much more serious than two minutes before. "You already are magic, sweetness. I don't mean the inherent power you have, but the beautiful person you are, with your strength, your grace, your charm, and your stalwart heart in the face of all that is so new and different for you. That's the magic here."

Wow. I'd never heard him talk like this. I sat up and took his hand. I wanted to kiss him but didn't want to remove Clara to do that. I gave his arm a tug and made him come to me. "I think that's supposed to be my line."

I pressed my lips to his and pushed my tongue along the seam of his mouth. He let me in, taking my tongue, giving what he knew I wanted. That was what we'd always done, give and take, take and give. With Clara though, we were something more. We could become one.

He broke the kiss before I was ready, but he never was a patient one. But he was right to do it. I didn't want Clara feeling left out. When I looked at her, the sparkling in her eyes was tenfold and she licked her own lips. "I love the way you love each other and I'm grateful I get to be a part of it with you."

Her heartfelt words meant so much to me, I couldn't even speak. Any words about how I was the one thankful that she was here with us were lost in my emotions. Tau did what he did best, and showed us both

"Clara, raise up on your knees a bit. I want to put Tau's cock into your hot cunt once again." Zucker was the one who gave her ripe ass a slap this time, and I thoroughly enjoyed the little oh her lips made and the blush on her cheeks. He reached between the two of us and found my cock, gave it a few hard strokes just to fucking tease me, and swiped my head up and down her slit, driving both me and Clara crazy.

Clara broke first. "Zucker if you keep it up, I will

forgo all my lessons in using my mouth on you and Tau and ask Leb and Nuss to let me pleasure them instead.

Zucker laughed. "Ah, but my sweet princess, I would enjoy watching you suck their cocks too. Especially if I was fucking either of them or you while you do it."

He punctuated his threat by spearing my cock into her waiting pussy but shoving two of his fingers in along with and scissoring them back and forth. Both Clara and I moaned. "And that, my loves, is just a taste of what's to come."

The same magic connecting the three of us began its delightful build up. I could already feel the zips and zings of sensation spurring Clara's arousal. Zucker and I had shared a bed with many a fae, but we'd never fucked a woman this way before. I wasn't sure if it was his anticipation or mine that had my heart fluttering in my chest.

I pulled Clara down for a kiss and took her mouth soft and slow. She was so incredibly precious to me and for the first time since I'd met Zucker, I was the one without words and needed to use my body to show her how I felt. Our tongued danced and even though I was supposed to be waiting for Zucker to slide his cock in, I couldn't help but thrust into her soft, wet pussy.

I ate up her little whimpers and decided I wanted to be kissing her when she came this time too. I'd take everything she had and keep it safe for as long as I could. Hopefully forever.

Zucker put a hand on my thigh and stilled my fucking. Clara and I both felt his cock head notch at her entrance. "Hold steady, you two. I'm going to push in nice and slow to let Clara's cunt get used to the stretch."

I pushed my hands into her hair and held her tight to me. Zucker pushed barely an inch in and the connection between all three skyrocketed to an even stronger level than before. The touch of pain Clara suffered as her channel stretched wider with two cocks inside of her, pushed her pleasure at the same time.

Having Zucker's cock slide along mine in such a tight space was like nothing I'd ever experienced. We'd been inside of each other before, we'd jacked the other off together, I'd sucked his cock while he sucked mine until we both came. None of it compared to this.

"That's it, sweetness, you can take us. I'm almost there. Fuck this is like a magical fucking fantasy." Zucker sank in as deep as he could go, and Clara's magic exploded around us. Blue and white and gold and red wisps sparkled through the air and perceptively wrapped us in a bubble of joy and wonder.

Our sensations were tripled again, no, even more. We were in each other's minds, bodies, but we had Leb and Nuss with us once again too. And that mysterious sixth consciousness, filling us all with more emotions of need and lust.

Because we were all so intertwined, when I moved, so did Zucker. Our cocks pressed into each other, sliding back and forth inside the squeeze of Clara's incredibly tight pussy. She groaned into my mouth, and I swallowed her every sound, returning it with a growl from deep within my spirit.

Nothing existed except our minds, our sensations, our bodies. We were one, all of us, and I finally belonged to someone so completely. More than just someone, five spirits tangled with my own and we would never be separated ever again.

I gently rocked my hips and let Zucker take over. He meted out a steady rhythm driving us closer and closer to that precipice of bliss. Faster and faster, he fucked us until the sweat beaded on upper lip and he had to make us come or the pleasure rippling in shock-waves around us would become unbearable.

"Just a little more, sweetness, you're almost there. Come on, let go, be mine, be ours." Zucker pleaded for Clara to come, for us both to give into his relentless fucking and explode.

What he didn't understand was that as tightly wound together as we all were, we couldn't come until he too let go. Only for him would I have broken my kiss with Clara. For him, I did, promising to taste her cries many more times in the future.

I caught Zucker's eyes with mine and though I was breathing hard, and could barely catch a breath to speak, I found the words he needed, finally able to say them and truly mean them. "I love you, Zucker Pflaume-Fee. I belong to you, in this circle of spirit and magic with our one true bonded mate. Let go and give yourself to us in return."

He knew the words before I even said them, and Clara echoed them in our minds. The first tight chord of her orgasm burst and Zucker followed her, letting himself love and be loved in return. His hot seed spilled into her first, and my cock and balls tightened, and I shot into her too.

When Zucker slowed, then stilled his thrusts, I slowly continued, mixing our essence inside of her our princess, and pushing it deep, hoping for new life. Even though it was unlikely until she was bonded with us all, I wanted her womb filled with both me and Zucker.

The three of us didn't move for a long time. We panted, and let our hearts race, slowing in their own time, still locked together in body and spirit. Zucker gave out a long exhale and then palmed the back of Clara's neck just as he had to me a million times. "I didn't know what love was until I was in your minds. I am not worthy, but I will strive to be every day."

She kissed me softly on the side of the mouth and we all felt it. Then she whispered. "You are worthy of love. Never let anyone tell you otherwise. I spent a lifetime letting others make me feel less than, and you've helped me understand that love doesn't work that way."

Zucker and I slid out of her body, and we reveled in the magical afterglow. Unlike before Clara's mind and body hummed in a new way. Instead of the slow fade like before, she closed her eyes and pulled her magic and spirit back into herself but leaving us with a piece of our spirits filled in with a part of hers.

The bond with both of us was now complete, and her magic could use and amplify our gifts. In two short days she was the most powerful magician in the Winter Realm. She had yet to find the Snowflake crown and consummate her bond with Nuss, so there was more power ready and waiting for her to yield.

She stood and gave Zucker the same kiss and then looked out across the grotto. "All five of you are worthy of my love."

But there were only four of us.

Until Konig walked into the grotto.

I'VE GOT YOU, UNDER MY SPELL

CLARA

When I lived in the human world, I don't think I ever truly knew what it felt like to be loved. So much of society told me that because of what I looked like, I wasn't worthy of romantic love.

Oh, I fell in love at the drop of a snowflake. There was always some boy at school, the guy who worked at the bookshop, some friend of my brothers. I didn't know how to not be in love. School girl crushes that ruled my every emotion.

As the years passed and my friends and the other girls I went to school and dance classes with found boyfriends and I didn't, the fearful realization sank in and entrenched itself. I would never get to experience for myself the rush of joy they so clearly felt when they were with their beloveds.

I didn't understand then the difference between unrequited love and the real thing. Because being loved in return was... magic.

I didn't understand that I couldn't find the right one for me because I wasn't in the right world.

I really didn't understand was that I wasn't destined to love and be loved by just one man - another tenant of the broken human society that told me I was wrong. Why did that world have to make love finite when it was so much grander?

Standing here in this special place where love was set to grow, I once again embraced my mission to show the Winter Realm how to love again. I was learning lessons in how to do it myself, but I was confident that once I'd fallen in love with and bonded with each of my true loves, that I could share that with the rest of the people here.

War and hate had no place in such a beautiful land.

I could help end that.

And I was going to start right now.

Consummating my bond with Zucker and Tau was so perfect and beautiful because not only did they love me, they loved each other. Their natural gifts of sensuality and empathy burst to life for all three of us, connected by my magic, and I couldn't have asked for a better present.

I could hardly wait until I got to join with all of

them at the same time. Each were so important to me in their own ways, but together we would be unstoppable. If any troop were to make this world ready for the return of the Vivandiere and the defeat of the Mouse Queen, it would be the six of us.

Yes. Six.

Leb gave me the courage to be a fierce warrior like him.

Tau helped me connect to my own buried fears and emotions and see that being together was better than isolation.

Zucker showed me that the only thing keeping me from being a strong, sexual woman was my own lack of self-confidence.

Nuss would be my forever protector and soon I would learn the lesson he had for me. Even with Tau's empathic connection, he was still guarding himself from me. But of them all, he knew and understood me the best. He was the one who had first-hand knowledge of how to access my magic. For that I would be ever grateful.

But it was Konig that I needed to bring back into the fold. While I didn't know or understood what happened to make him their enemy, I could sense the deep betrayal felt on both sides. I should wait until I'd bonded with Nuss, to try my first bid at repairing old wounds with love. But then I'd miss the opportunity to heal them sooner rather than later.

Konig was here now. He'd been with us half the

night. If he was going to attack and hurt or kill anyone, it would have been easiest when we were otherwise busy. But he wasn't here to do that. He wanted in. To our lives and our hearts.

Because his was broken.

I was going to fix it.

Konig dropped down from his hiding place, where he'd watched the three of us consummate our bond and had joined in spilling his own seed just as Leb and Nuss had over on the shore. I felt him the instant I connected with Tau. But I'd known all along he was with us.

"Hello, princess. Have a good fucking?" Konig strode toward me as if on an afternoon stroll and he saw a pretty flower he wanted to pluck.

I opened my arms to him but Tau and Zucker jumped in front of me. Zucker had grabbed his daggers from his clothes, and he held them out pointing at Konig's head. "Stop right there, bastard. This is no place for a rat."

"Maybe not, but I think the mouse army would enjoy this warm oasis." Konig snapped his fingers and hundreds of mice swarmed up from around his feet, dropped from the ceiling, and popped out of every plant and flower.

"Konig, stop. We don't have to fight." I didn't yell, I didn't scream, I didn't even cringe at the sight of all the tiny animals. They were a part of him, and his own special gift and I was no longer afraid.

"Oh, but I'm afraid we do. You see, I am bound to follow the Mouse Queen's orders and she wants me to bring you to her." He spat when he talked of the queen.

The mice swirled around my feet, but never touched me. Zucker and Tau weren't so lucky. I don't know how, but the mice wrapped the two of them up in what had to be miles and miles of grass and vines so that they couldn't even move. The bindings covered their mouths and though they grunted and tried to shout, their words were distorted and muffled.

I grabbed and scratched at the cords, ripping, and tearing, but there was always another and another mouse to replace anything I tore away. Tau shook his head at me and the uselessness of trying to free them surged into my gut. I gave up and turned back to Konig ready to beg him to let them go. But when I saw the pain buried in his eyes, I changed plans.

"Then I unbind you. You don't belong to her, but you and I do belong to each other." I'd felt the link between us the first time I saw him. He felt it too.

Konig's eyes went dark and his whole face matched. "If only it was that simple. Even you with your magic and spirit cannot break this curse."

He strode toward me and for the first time, I was afraid of him. Had I been so mistaken? I was sure love would conquer all. But it wasn't even showing up for the fight. An angry, grim Konig advanced on me.

The temperature in the grotto dropped and the moisture in the air froze. Millions of snowflakes formed before my very eyes. A huge crack sounded and whirled around to look toward the source at the shore, Nuss had his sword shoved into the water's edge and a thick layer of ice ran across the warm lake toward the island.

The power of the Land of Snowflakes at work.

Leb had somehow called down a reindeer from outside and was riding on the back of one like knight in shining armor coming to my rescue. His axe was over head, and it looked as though he was going to hurl it at Konig.

This was all going so, so wrong.

I threw myself in front of Konig, my arms sprawled wide in defense, and Leb roared out at me. "Clara, don't, move."

Konig grabbed me around the waist, pulling my bum tight against his front. He lowered his face, scraping his scuff against my skin, and kissed my neck. "Yes, do as your Viking says. Don't move, or they'll all suffer. My army are here only to capture you, but they can be set to kill just as easily."

I froze as still as the air and ice. "I can't let you injure them, because I see you, my Mouse Prince, it would be the same as hurting me or yourself.

He scowled at me and snapped his fingers once again. The mice spewed forth from the island across the newly formed ice, building a bridge with their bodies up and over it. Konig shoved me toward the living bodies bridge. I shoved him right back. "What are you doing? This isn't right. We can defeat the mouse queen together."

"With your little band of rebels, princess? They've lied to you, just as they did to me. They only want what is best for themselves and their lands. You'll soon see." He grabbed one of Zucker's fallen daggers and pointed it at me this time. "Now, move."

Leb was almost here and Nuss was right behind him, sliding across the ice like he was on skates. I needed to stall for just a little bit of time. If the four of them could band together, we could capture Konig and make him see the light. "Can't I please get my clothes? I'm so cold."

"No, no. I'm thoroughly enjoying watching your tits and ass jiggle," Konig gave me a shove and I was forced to step onto the first writhing stair of the bridge made of mice. "Although not as much as I'll relish it when I'm fucking you and you're calling only my name as you come on my cock, just as you for did Leb and Zucker, and Tau."

I refused to think of his words as a threat. Mostly because I did want him to claim me in the same way the other had.

Leb leaped from the reindeer onto the island and Nuss was coming up under the bridge. I just needed to keep him talking a little longer. "You won't be able to do that if you give me to the Mouse Queen."

Konig spun and threw the dagger, not at Leb, but at Zucker. Leb dove in front of the blade, taking it in the shoulder to save his friend. Konig took advantage of that and rushed me, grabbing me by the arm and hauling me further up the bridge. "I'll turn you in to her, but not until I'm obligated to on the twelfth day of Christmas. Until then you're mine and I'll do with you what I like."

"Princess, jump. I'll catch you." Nuss was directly below us and he held his good arm aloft toward me.

I had no doubt even with just one working arm, he would catch me, but I couldn't let Konig escape, even if it meant I did. He was supposed to be with us, not working against me and his brethren. I ripped my elbow from Konig's grip, but not to run away. I had to pray that the others would understand what I did next and didn't think I was betraying them.

I did what I hoped was the last thing the dark warrior before me would expect. I pushed my hands into his hair and pressed my lips to his, kissing him with everything I had.

To my relief, he responded by wrapping and arm around my waist and the other across my back and kissed me back. This wasn't like the quick kiss he'd stolen from me in the Christmas Tree Forest. This was passionate, and needy, and my magic responded to something so much more than lust from him.

I could taste, and feel, and sense the love hidden deep in his heart. It was there, it was for me, and I was going to save him by bringing it out. My magic swirled up and I called on the gifts from the others to help me.

I poured all my newfound sensuality into this kiss, and felt his emotions respond in kind. His heart was walled up so tight, yet inside that wall was a warrior's spirit fighting for what he thought was righteous. If he was bad or evil, he wouldn't care, but above all, that's the gift I felt in him, that I connected to with my magic.

He cared so deeply, it physically hurt.

The intensity of Konig's emotions being bared to me overwhelmed my senses. Suddenly, I felt like I was tumbling, caught up maelstrom of magic and lust. Oh, oh God, I was falling. The mouse bridge beneath our feet was collapsing, and we were caught up in a literal tornado of mice, swirling around us and carrying us across the ice and then up the tunnel to the cave entrance.

We emerged back out into the snow and freezing temperatures, just as the sun was setting. We'd been down in the grotto the entire day, secluded in our little world of love and bonding. The harsh reality of my situation hit me as a cold slap in the face.

"You can't control me with the promise of your body. You already belong to me, at least for the next few days. I'll take you when and how I like, and you'll be begging me for more, not the other way around." He marched me over to the waiting sleigh, minus one reindeer.

"You know that's not what I was trying to do."

I wasn't going to save Konig by convincing him to open his heart and rejoin the fold of the princes born under the Christmas Star. He was taking me away from them. I shivered, only partially from being bare to this snowy world. I'd really screwed up and had no one to blame but myself.

I wasn't going to cry or beg or play the victim. The warrior magic in me wouldn't allow that, even if old human Clara was already doing all three of those inside. I wrapped my arms around myself, straightened my spine, and held my chin up high.

What I was going to do was fix the problem I'd just made. The way I'd been trying to reach him so far was all wrong. Appealing to the good in him would have to wait until I'd chipped away some of the layers he had built around his heart. How to get him to see reason wasn't entirely clear to me. I needed some of Nuss's good old know how and understanding of my magic.

Then like I'd conjured him up, Nuss was here. The mouse tornado deposited him and the missing reindeer next to the sleigh. Except it wasn't my magic that brought him here tied up and gagged.

"Get in before you freeze to death. I don't fuck dead princesses." Konig secured the reindeer back into its harness and pointed to the seat of the sleigh. "Your dress and some warm blankets are in the bench. Get dressed and ready to go."

He grabbed Nuss and pushed him up against the side of the vehicle. Nuss did his best to put up a fight, but the bindings didn't allow him to do much but wiggle like a worm. It didn't take him more than a minute to maneuvered Nuss into the floor of the back seat. The whole time I stood there looking like a fool with my stomach falling so hard and fast it was a worse feeling than being in the avalanche.

I'd led us right into his scheme by coercing the men to take this sleigh. It had come from Konig, and it was all a set up for this. "What are you going to do to Nuss? You don't need him, leave him be. Just take me."

Konig rounded on me, and that dark look was back on his face. My heart skipped one beat, then two as I froze, my fight or flight instincts completely scared into submission. "You have no idea what I need. If you did, you would have come with me three days ago. Nuss knows that and I'm sure he's spun quite the tale of his chivalry and courage while painting me out to be the mud that dirties his boots."

It was hard to force my voice out in the face of Konig's anger, but I managed a whisper. "He hasn't, I swear it."

"Don't lie to me to save him. Of course he has. There was a time I thought a Snowflake could have good in them, but he proved me wrong. Now get the fuck in the sleigh before I tie you up. Unless that's what you like, pretty princess."

I still couldn't move.

He eyed me up and down and his eyes flickered over my bum, that was red from more than just the cold. "I already know you like to be watched, you like a little pain with your pleasure, and you enjoyed that spanking you got. I'm willing to bet you're getting wet right now thinking of me binding your wrists over your head and making you kneel on the floor for me."

Nuss made a series of noises that I was quite sure were threats to Konig's life, but he couldn't do anything for me now. Because Konig was right. I did want him to take control.

I wanted him to tell me exactly what to do to pleasure him, and how to do it, and when, and where. None of the same thoughts had even crossed my mind when I was with Leb, or Zucker, or Tau.

My magic rose up and sparkles of blue swirled around the two of us. It drew Konig to me and he shoved his hand into my hair and gripping a clump of it tight, tipping my head back so I could do nothing but look up at him. The second he touched me again, I understood what his gift was.

He had the power to command.

OF MICE AND MAGIC

KONIG

*S*he was mine.

The fabled lost princess of the Land of Spirit and Magic, born under the Christmas Star along with me and six other princes, had finally returned to the Winter Realm, and she belonged to me.

At least for the next eight days. The Mouse Queen would have my head when and if she found out that I had the princess and hadn't immediately brought her to the castle, but that was her own damn fault for not being more specific.

I may have to obey her commands, but only in the extremely specific way that the curse demanded. The queen hadn't specified when I had to bring Clara to her, only that I had until the twelfth day of Christmas. That gave me plenty of time.

Surely if she could fall in love with the rest of the Nutcracker guard in two days, I could get her to fall in love with me in a week and see exactly how they had all betrayed the meek of the realm instead of protecting them.

If she didn't see how the other lands had mistreated my people, than she was just as corrupt as the rest of them. I wasn't yet ready to accept that such pure magic and spirit could look the other way at the atrocities wrought on the inhabitants of the Land of Animals, but I'd been wrong about those I believed in before.

Clara looked at me like she was both scared and turned-on at the same time. Perhaps she was. For being a naive virgin when she'd entered the Winter Realm, she'd grabbed onto her sexual desires like a fiercer warrior than I could have foreseen.

She was so much more than any of us expected.

"Don't make me tell you again to get dressed and sit down, or so much more than that spanking you so desire is what will be waiting for you when we get to our destination." She had to be fucking freezing and yet she still stood her ground.

"I... don't want you to spank me." We both knew she did. Her pink ass had color in it not from the cold but from Tau and Zucker's hands.

Stars above she was fucking glorious standing here

in her naked glory, defenseless and yet still fighting. She was the champion my people needed on their side.

"Yes, you do. And I will do that and so much more to pleasure you, princess." As would the good prince of the Snowflakes. He just didn't know it yet.

Out of us all, he thought he knew the most about how her magic worked. Nuss was sure, only he could control Clara and bend her magic to his will. The Snowflake court and their all-knowing church decided they were the gatekeepers of all the knowledge left over after the destruction of the Land of Magic and Spirit. But what they didn't know was that the behind those forbidden walls, was not simply eviscerated grounds destroyed in the battle between good and evil. The Steel Tree Castle still stood, and within its ruins was all I needed to learn.

A beautiful blush rose up her chest and cheeks. Wasn't I going to have fun bringing that out in her over and over? But along with that flush came a defiance that made me want her all the more. "You can't tell me what I do and do not want."

She clasped her fists at her side and the magic swirling around us turned into a snow flurry, obscuring her from my view for just a moment. She forgot, or perhaps didn't understand that the beast in me didn't need sight to track her every move. My other senses served me just as well.

When she tried to make a run for the Flower Fae border, I was ready.

"Hey, hey, you flower people assassins up there, help me." She shouted toward the trees where the guards had their arrows trained on us.

The only thing those Flower Fae were going to shoot at were Sweet Fae trying to cross the border. They hadn't even flinched at the mouse army surrounding this cave entrance since it was on the Land of Sweet's side. Probably happy I was invading the Sugar Plum Court.

I heard their bow strings stretch at the ready. Shit. Had they figured out what an advantage it would be to have the princess in their land? They had seen Tau enter the cave with her and yet not return. I had no doubt they had their spies headed into the cave from the Land of Flowers side now and that meant a rescue mission for at least Leb and Tau.

Enough. I wasn't losing the small advantage I had over the Nutcrackers.

I captured the princess, and this time didn't give her a choice. I threw her over my shoulder and held her arms and feet in a soldier's carry. No amount of squirming would allow her to escape me.

"I don't want to hurt you, my lady, but I will if I have to." In the service of my people, I would sacrifice her strong will and her comfort.

In hauling her back to the sleigh, I caught Nuss's glare. He would hate me even more in the coming days. That was nothing new. He thrashed against his bindings and made a series of sounds that were likely cursing my name.

I was already cursed. His wouldn't hurt me any more than the Queen's.

For a half second, I considered throwing her in the back seat with him, just to show her that she had no power in this situation. She might have some access to her magic, but without her bond to the Snowflake Prince, she wouldn't be able to use it to her full ability yet.

The draw to have her by my side as we raced to the castle was more than I could resist, even if she'd be a pain in my ass the whole way. I dropped her onto the seat, loathe to let her skin escape my touch. Once we got to our destination, I'd keep the rooms nice and warm so I could keep her naked the whole time. But until then, I wouldn't have her freeze to death.

"We don't have time for you to dress now." I yanked the pile of soft woven blankets out and tossed them onto her lap. "Wrap yourself in these from head to toe, and if you move even and inch from that bench, I'll strap you down for the duration of our ride with my belt."

She did something I didn't expect even a little bit in response. She stuck her tongue out at me. Such adorable defiance.

"I can think of a lot better things I'd like you to do with your tongue, but they'll have to wait." I sat next to her and took up the reigns, thought I didn't need them.

With nothing more than a push of my thoughts, I sent the reindeer the mental map of our route to the Christmas Tree Forest and then across to the border of the Land of Spirit and Magic. We'd skirt along the far side where the once thriving jewel of the Winter Realm met the wild Land of Animals.

They took off like an arrow, and the princess squeaked beside me. She glanced back toward the cave, but no one was coming to rescue her. My army would keep the other Nutcrackers busy until we were far away.

I didn't count on the Flower Fae to take any notice of us. In fact, I'd assumed the opposite. The first arrows landed hard into the side of the sleigh. Those were only warning shots because their assassins didn't miss.

"Get down, and stay down, princess. We've just been marked as enemies of the DewDrop Court." We'd have to risk going deeper into Sweet Fae territory if we were going to avoid getting shot. I could take and arrow or two, but I didn't want the reindeer hurt.

"Oh my God, why are they shooting at us? I'm on their side." She ducked as another volley slammed into the path ahead of us to tear up the runners and knock us off course. My nimble reindeer avoided them easily, but I feared the next round would be aimed at them.

The countryside was hilly and riddled with caves where the sugar was mined. Only one led back to the tunnels under the castle. I'd snuck through before but didn't dare risk that again. It was the Christmas Tree

Forest or bust. I steered the sleigh into the candy cane trees to obscure the line of sight for anyone shooting at us and spurred the team to go faster than ever before. We were practically flying already, but they found a little more speed for me.

They too understood our cargo and what was at stake.

"No one but Flower Fae are on their side. They hate everyone, including you and me, and your snowflake pal." If Tau was discovered injured, there was already a death sentence on my head. Still only warning shot arrows came at us. We were far enough from the border between the two fae lands now that they shouldn't be able to reach us. Unless this incident broke the current treaty and the Flower Fae had just invaded.

I mentally checked in with the mice I'd left behind in the grotto. Sure enough, they were swarming around Flower Fae who'd snuck in from the entrance on their side of the border to rescue Tau. The DewDrop Court up until now spent most of their military resources on their long-standing civil war with the Sweet Fae.

The Mouse Queen would not like that I'd stirred that nest of stinging nettles. That was something I'd deal with later. Hopefully much, much later with Clara by my side.

Unless I did something drastic right here, right now, we were never going to make it to the Steel Tree

Castle, much less the Christmas tree forest. "Princess, it's time to share some of that magic of yours with me."

She stared at me wide-eyed and worried. From the fear written there, she knew her blood could give someone access to her magic. Not even the Mouse Queen knew that. I shouldn't either. But I knew a lot of things I wasn't supposed to.

I'd bet the Prince of Snowflakes and his damn Church of the Christmas Star did. If he'd fucking hurt her, I was going to kill him. Slowly.

Fuck. I knew that avalanche was too big to only have been triggered by the Gingerbread Vikings booby trap on the mountain. Nuss had access to both the prince and princess that day. He'd probably been drunk on having access to all that power to destroy me.

"I'm not going to hurt you, Clara. But those assassins will." I pushed the blanket around her shoulders back just enough to grab onto those soft blonde curls and twist them around my fist. "Open your heart to me as you have the Nutcracker Guard, and I can save us from a painful death."

The kisses I'd stolen from her before were about lust and power, not a connection. She needed a bond to let her magic flow. Now was a shitty time to ask for that, but I was running out of options.

"Kidnapping me is not the way to win my heart, Konig." There was steel in her words, just as in her spine. She truly was a Stahlbaum. Once again, she surprised the shit out of me, for when I'd determined to kiss her and steal any bit of magic that rose up, Clara leaned in and brushed her lips over mine. Then she whispered, "So I guess I'll have to win yours."

She wrapped her arms around my shoulders and kissed me, pouring her magic into my very spirit. My skin tingled from the inside out, my cock went so hard I thought I might come in my pants, and the world around us became so still and perfect that it was like a painting hanging on the wall of a castle.

I could kiss her forever.

Or I could save our lives.

For one more second, I let the magic seep into my cells, felt it take over as far as I could allow it, and then I broke our kiss. With all the force I could muster, I pushed the magic out, along with my mental command to the team pulling the sleigh. "Let's see if reindeer really know how to fly."

I gave a snap to the reins and the world around us slowed like a frozen night. The reindeers' hooves pounded along the ground and then into the air. Their breath freezing on each exhale puffed in the sky, higher and higher, and the sleigh slipped off the ice as if it weighed nothing at all.

"How are you doing this?" Clara looked down to the ground falling away below us and gripped the side of the sleigh with both her hands.

"I'm not. You are. I only told the animals what do to with the magic at their disposal." Clara stared back at me with all the sweet naivety of someone who hasn't been hurt by betrayal and war. It would be so easy to love her.

If only everything in my life was different, I would do exactly that. But no amount of magic could break the curse on my heart and so I'd have to live with hoping she could at least break the curse on our land and my people.

Nuss floundered around in the back seat and made way too much noise. "Careful there, captain, or you'll end up a falling snowflake."

"Where are you taking us?"

I wished we could fly straight to the Land of Spirit and Magic, but there was only one way through the magical barrier placed around the eviscerated land and it wasn't by air. "We'll land in the Christmas Tree Forest, then you'll have to trust me. You'll want to see what I have to show you."

"Just tell me."

"To even speak the words aloud is forbidden." The queen had told me never to call that place by its name, and I could do nothing but obey.

"You're taking me home, aren't you?" Her spirit twirled in her bright blue eyes like a ballerina.

Somehow, I knew she didn't mean to the human world. She understood now who she was, and that would make it all the harder for her to see how her land had been destroyed by greed and fear. "Yes."

I turned away from her and scowled out at the final rays of the sun setting behind the Gingerbread mountains. I was letting myself be too soft with her. This was a harsh world she'd come back to, and kindness and love were the last thing on my agenda.

I needed her to fight for the throne, and to save my people from the tyranny of the Mouse Queen. Falling in love with her was the last thing either of us needed. The Nutcracker Guard thought bonding with her as consorts was the way to get her on their sides.

She didn't need to be loved or love in return, she simply needed a crown and a good fucking. With the four dangling around her neck and the one I'd stolen, she'd be the most powerful princess of the Land of Spirit and Magic this realm had ever seen.

Seven crowns would be better, but five would have to do.

We were just coming over the edge of the Christmas Tree Forest and Clara pointed down. "Look, is... is that Fritz running through the snow?"

I always knew some of the Queen's loyal mice were in my army. They'd pledged fealty to her under coercion just as I had. When I'd sent the mouse army to attack the SugarPlum Court, I knew some were on a special assignment to find the queen's pet and return him.

While they were loyal to her, they were still under my command, and I could see and feel their thoughts. Even if I couldn't control them, she couldn't hide their mission from me.

Clara pointed again. "It is him, and he's got my marzipan pixies in a cage. We have to stop him."

A day ago, the queen couldn't care less about this wayward prince. He'd proven to be nothing but a spoiled brat with no magical talent hidden within. Nothing like Clara's natural ability. But still, he was of the Steel Tree Court and his blood was just as hers. Powerful to someone who knew how to wield it.

If she wanted him back now, well, I didn't want to consider the consequences. If we stopped and tried to get him, I would have to fight my own army. If we didn't, it became a race to see who could learn to utilize the lost magic.

I wouldn't hurt any of my own people. Ever. I was simply going to have to bet that I had a better shot at accessing Clara's magic with the broken pieces of the crown and the connection I would forge with her. If that didn't work, I'd convince her by letting her see the dire circumstances of the Land of Animals firsthand.

"No, your pixies will have to be one more sacrifice in this war. We can't let your brother even see us."

"What? No. We have to save them." Clara struggled to move away from me, but I wasn't letting her anywhere near the edge of the sleigh where she could fall.

I wrapped my arm around her and let her squirm and even punch me in the chest. None of that hurt me. The tears pooling at her lashes tore me to pieces. I'd survived worse.

"They're my friends. I have to help them."

I directed the reindeer to turn away from Fritz's path toward the Land of Animals. We could circle the outer edge of the forest to get to the place we could slip into her land. Until then I'd have to mouse up and ignore her tears. "You'll help them and everyone else in this forsaken realm when you usurp the Mouse Queen."

Clara looked up at me and those tears fell, forming icicle trails on her cheeks. "You've got the wrong girl."

THE LAND OF SPIRIT, MAGIC, AND DESTRUCTION

CLARA

*K*onig was nothing that I'd thought he would be.

Dark and handsome, sure. Lustful and made my belly go all a flutter. Yep.

An asshole who would hurt those closest to me or let them be harmed. That I hadn't seen coming.

Which was really stupid of me. He'd been trying to kidnap me from the moment we met. Him with a sword in his hand and doing his best to kill my protector. What in the hell was wrong with me? I couldn't believe I'd been so stupid and so incredibly wrong about him.

Or that I'd thought I could save him.

All he cared about was usurping the Mouse Queen. Why couldn't any of them see that I couldn't do that. I wasn't the Vivandiere. They needed a real warrior, a woman who could lead them in battle.

All I knew how to do was dance and my newly acquired wanton skill of having sex with men I'd met only a few days ago. Maybe Fritz was right, and I was just a whore.

No. Nope. Absolutely not. It didn't matter that I hadn't known Leb, Zucker, or Tau for exceedingly long, we were destined to be together. I had a deep and meaningful connection with each of them. We were in love.

L.

O.

V.

E.

Love. That's how I was going to help the Winter Realm. I knew that all the way to my spirit and back.

I was hurting right now because Konig hadn't fallen in line with my plans like a good little boy. What had I expected? That one kiss from me would cure all his darkness?

Sort of. Yeah.

I'd also thought that the Land of Sweets and the Land of Flowers sounded like nice places filled with nice people. Not spies, intrigue, and poisoned arrows.

God, I hoped Leb, Zucker, and Tau were alright. I could survive anything if they were alive. At least I had

Nuss. It was entirely my fault we were in this situation, but I was above telling him I was sorry. He'd gone awfully quiet back there. I hoped he was working on an escape plan.

"Hold on to something. I've never landed a flying sleigh pulled by eight reindeer before." The ground rose closer and closer, and I considered jumping at the last minute and mad dashing off to find Fritz... and beat him senseless with the cage after I freed my pixies. What did he want with them anyway?

There was the small matter of my not having any clothes or shoes one. The blankets Konig gave me were fine while we were sitting in the sleigh, but no doubt I'd leave them strewn along the snow the second I tried to run from him.

Not to mention, I'd seen him move. He was faster than a flea. I'd get all of ten steps before he caught up to me, and then I knew there would be hell to pay.

In spankings.

Dammit. I shouldn't still be turned on by him. I was blaming Zucker's sex magic for that.

Sigh. No, I was not. I had a connection with Konig, just like I did with the others. No matter how wrong it might be, I already had feelings for him that I couldn't deny.

That meant to me that he couldn't be all bad. I just needed to be more careful about what I let him get away with from now on.

The sleigh bumped down into the snow and the

reindeer didn't miss a beat. They just kept on running, dragging us along behind them. The trees in this part of the forest were even more dense and getting thicker by the moment.

A branch smacked me in the face. "Ouch. Can't we slow down?"

"No, we're getting close." Konig growled and focused entirely on the path ahead. The sun had finally fully set, and the forest was dark. Darker than where I'd first landed with Nuss. None of the trees here were lit up and there certainly weren't any marzipan pixies to make the place joyful.

I peered into the darkness, trying to see anything. I felt it before I saw it. Tingles of magic danced across my skin and the little red crown charm my mother had left me lit up, glowing from within.

But there was something wrong. The sparks of magic didn't feel anything like I'd experienced before. They flickered and fritzed out before I could truly feel their warmth. A lump formed in my throat and when I tried to swallow it down, I got a boulder sitting at the bottom of my stomach.

"What happened here?" My words were barely more than a whisper.

"This won't be easy for you, but I need you to suck it up." The sleigh finally slowed to a stop and Konig jumped out. The animals were restless and jumpy. He unclipped their harnesses, and one by one, they dashed off into the forest. They were getting far away from here as fast as possible.

I wanted to do the same. My chest literally ached like I was having a heart attack. But I knew that's not what it was. Whatever was tearing up my heart was coming from the other side of that darkness. "I can't go in there."

Nuss jumped up behind me, holding one of Zucker's daggers at the ready in his good hand. "And you won't have to, ever. No one should be subjected to the atrocities in there. Now get behind me, princess. Konig and I have an old score to settle."

I knew he was too quiet back there. I climbed over the seat, but I didn't miss the anger flashing in Konig's eyes as I did so. I shook my head at him and looked away. "I can't, Konig. There's something terribly wrong in there. I thought you said you were taking me home."

"I have. Welcome to what's left of the Land of Spirit and Magic, Princess Clara." Konig bowed and behind him a gash of burning red rent the darkness open from the tops of the trees to the ground.

From inside, a melody played, a tune I almost remembered. It softly called to me, and I stepped from the sleigh. Men and women danced gracefully through my memory, and someone held me safe, but far away and long ago. I could almost remember, but the images faded like embers in this fiery gash.

My heart yearned to remember even as it ached. I had to know.

"Clara, no. You don't know what's in there. Stop." Nuss reached for me, but I pushed his arm away.

My legs didn't heed Nuss any mind. Where once I was scared, now I was mesmerized. It didn't matter that I was in bare feet in the snow, I felt no cold. I walked right past Konig and toward the gash. The closer I got the hotter my own crown charm burned as if it was an important part of that fire but coming from inside of me. It was glowing as bright as the tear in the world in front of me.

I reached my hand out and the magic inside of me swirled up. It had been a beautiful blue color when I'd been with my men, but now it matched the red light of this strange place. "Is this a portal? Like the one I came through to get here?"

Konig stepped up beside me on my right, and Nuss on my left. "No, Clara, it isn't. This shouldn't even exist. You mustn't go in there."

"She needs to see what happened to our world. Let her go." Konig's voice still carried his anger, but the magic here seemed to suck it up.

"You don't know what's on the other side. The Land of Spirit and Magic was destroyed. That's why this barrier is here. There's nothing there for you to see," Nuss argued. "I can't let you."

"Why don't you see for yourself, Nutcracker." Konig jumped behind both of us and shoved us into the glowing gash.

I spun and grabbed both Nuss's hand and Konig's

shirt, dragging him with us at the last moment before we fell through the broken barrier.

My mind exploded with images of armies marching through the snow, animals being whipped while pulling machines of war behind them, Fae men and women murdering each other, and Viking axes smashing buildings, bodies, and everything else in their path.

The most ruthless of all were the magicians. They used their magic to tear people asunder, to make anyone who opposed them fall to their knees in pure agony until their heads exploded and feasted on the bodies of the animals that lain slain in the fields.

All but the Vivandiere — the Queen of Spirit and Magic, of the Steel Tree court. She was no longer the young woman who'd hidden the broken crowns around the realm on her adventures. She was a mother, a queen, and a magician. Instead of fighting in senseless fighting she'd tried to prevent, she took her children and disappeared, lost to the war.

I fell on my hands and knees into a pile of rubble. The broken pebbles scraped my hands, and only the thick blankets wrapped around me, saved my knees. I couldn't breathe, I couldn't hear with all the high-pitched buzzing in my ears.

I turned my face to the side and vomited into a burned skeleton of a long dead plant in a broken pot. When I looked away to wipe my mouth, I saw the ruins of a once great castle. It was the only thing left standing in a barren wasteland.

There was no snow, but it was bitter cold, and the wind blew relentlessly. This... this is what was left of my home. Nothing but horrific memories and the relics of hubris.

Konig and Nuss tumbled through the gash a breath later and behind them, the rip in the barrier closed. Where it had been was now only more destruction as far as I could see. The two of them quickly rolled to their feet and Nuss punched Konig in the face.

It didn't take long before they were shouting slurs at each other and doing their best to beat the other into a bloody mess. I couldn't stand it.

I stood and held out my hands, drawing on the latent magic energy still in the ground, air, and ashes here. My voice boomed and echoed, "Stop."

They both froze and looked over at me as if I'd grown three heads. "No more fighting. No. More."

I turned my back on them and stumbled away, toward the only shelter from the biting wind. Small chunks of the castle remained, and someone had put a blanket across a tattered archway to serve as a door and windbreak.

"Clara, wait." Nuss ran after me, but I didn't stop for him.

I shoved my way into the stone room and found carpets, a bed, a fireplace stacked with wood, and provisions on a shelf. I hobbled toward the shelf and grabbed up a jug filled with pungent liquid. I didn't care what it was. I needed to rinse out my mouth and get my bearings.

Nuss and came flying into the room, Konig on top of him, wrestling him to the wall. What I hadn't noticed were the steel shackles bolted into the wall.

"I said no more fighting." I could hardly get the words out. Everything had drained out of me, even though I'd absorbed energy from this place. That wasn't exactly right. It was more like tired after eating and drinking too much. I was both full of that latent energy and exhausted from it.

Konig shoved Nuss up against the wall and clasped his good hand into one of the manacles. Nuss wasn't even fighting back. Konig then grabbed his broken arm, tearing the sling away, and closing the other on his bad wrist. Nuss cried out but gritted his teeth. I didn't even have the wherewithal to go to him.

I would do what I could to heal him as soon as I rested a little.

"My apologies, my lady." Konig gave me a little bow. "We weren't fighting. I was simply apprehending this enemy of the realm."

I lifted the jug to my lips and took a long gulp of potent wine. I'd meant to take a small sip, but I was suddenly so thirsty. Konig came over and gently lowered the jug, carefully taking it from me. "I'll not have you drowning your sorrows and getting drunk on me."

I knew I shouldn't, but I leaned into him and laid my head on his shoulder. Even if his was the only arms available to me, I needed this small comfort. Everything was wrong, it was all broken. This wasn't how the stories Drosselmeyer told to me and Fritz ended.

Konig stiffened at first, but then he wrapped his arms around me. "I'm afraid this is only the beginning of the harsh lessons I have for you, princess."

"Don't you touch her, you bastard. We could be out there saving the realm from your greedy mother if you hadn't betrayed us. Let us go so we can get back to the duty you gave up on." Nuss hadn't ever sounded so enraged before. He was the calm, cool, and collected captain of the Nutcracker Guard. My hero, my protector.

Now when he needed me to save him, I couldn't. I didn't have anything left in me. I peered out at him and saw so much pain written in lines around his mouth and eyes. I mouthed the words I didn't have the energy to say to him. "I'm sorry."

"You're the one who gave up on me." Konig's words were controlled and measured. Though he addressed Nuss, he looked at me, lifting my chin so I had to meet his eyes. "I never stopped fighting for what was right, but you did, Captain."

"You turned on us and allied yourself with the fucking Mouse Queen." Nuss yanked against his chains. "The same woman who destroyed everything around us. I didn't give up on you. You forgot who and what you are."

"Never." He whispered that last word and then lifted me into his arms. In just a few long strides, he crossed to the bed and laid me down. I know exactly who I am. Consort to the Queen of Spirit and Magic."

He took my hand and kissed it. "Long live the Queen."

A COLD SNOWFLAKE

NUSS

I couldn't believe I'd fucking let this happen. I'd failed the princess and the entire Winter Realm by letting Konig steal her away from us when we were only one crown away from becoming the strongest bonded court in the history of our world.

I'd failed so utterly that if I wasn't so damn angry, I'd be ready to give up. The fire burning through my veins where my cool ice of a Snowflake Prince should be had me ready to tear the fucking chains out of this stone wall and strangle him where he slept beside my beautiful princess. Except I couldn't. This damned broken arm had me literally handicapped.

I slammed my good fist against the stone, and it

hardly even made a sound. Never had I been in any place as desolate and bare as the ruins of the former Steel Tree Castle. Of course, I knew the land was demolished in the Mouse Queen's final attack, but this was so far beyond what I thought it would be like.

It hurt to even imagine how many lives and how much magic was lost here.

I couldn't allow Clara to stay here any longer than we already were. The sorrow seeping out of the land would eventually affect her and it could taint her magic. We needed her to be pure of magic and spirit just as she was now. Or how she was an hour ago before Konig had gotten his claws into her.

She was already drained. I saw the internal hurt in her spirit when she couldn't help me. Fuck. She shouldn't ever have to help me. It was my job to protect her. I was the captain of the Nutcracker Guard for Christmas' sake. I was doing a shitty ass job of giving her what she wanted and needed so far.

I couldn't even help give her the pleasure that would unlock her magic. She was never going to fall in love with me.

All the fantasies I'd had of the two of us searching out and finding the snowflake crown together and then consummating our bond in the most perfect of ways were gone. I was going to die here in the hell of the seven realms, never having experienced the pleasures of the flesh.

And what for?

Because the Church of the Christmas Star thought I was some kind of messiah? Because the king and queen of the Land of Snowflakes believed them and hadn't treated me like a son my entire life.

Fuck them.

If I had to do this whole thing over again, I'd have been right there in bed with Clara and the others that very first night.

Clara groaned in her sleep, and I strained against the chains keeping me from her. Konig was consummating his bond with her. No, that was a lie to myself. He was fucking her, enjoying her body, and showing her the pleasure I had not. Jealousy, guilt, and self-recriminations stoked the fire burning in my blood.

He had every damned right to bond with her and savor the flavor of her cunt or sink his cock into her tight heat if she so chose him — he too was born under the Christmas Star.

"Shh. Settle the fuck down. She's just having a dream, asshole." Konig sat up from their little love nest and glared at me. "If you wake her, I'll kill you where you stand. She needs rest."

He crawled out of the blankets, stoked the fire keeping this hellhole warm, and sauntered over to me. "You thought I was fucking her, didn't you?"

I turned my face away. He would still know. He always had seen and understood me better than anyone else. Back in the days when we were all on the same side, he'd been my friend and confidant. His betrayal was the hot coals churning the fire in my blood.

Konig circled around, stalking me like the predator he was. He swiped his thumb across his mouth and then sucked the end of it as if it was covered in the most delicious nectar. "She is delicious and it's your own damn fault you haven't tasted her yet."

"You haven't either." He couldn't have. I would know. Whether she and I had bonded and consummated or not, we were connected. But here in the destruction of the Land of Spirit and Magic maybe everything was different. Clara was already broken. "I can feel her magic when she is aroused."

"Haven't I?" He smiled so smugly that I wanted to punch his teeth out. "Why do you think she sleeps so soundly now? I gave her the comfort and escape she needed."

"She doesn't need shit from you." I had so much more to say, but it wouldn't do me any good to argue with him. He had all the power, and I had none. How the tables had turned.

"Perhaps I can decide what I need and from whom." Clara approached us, her hair wild, her cheeks flushed from sleep, and only a blanket wrapped around her plump body.

Shit. "My lady, my apolo—"

"Not now, and not here." Konig grabbed Clara and held her, so she faced me, his arms wrapped around her waist and her throat. "Until you're ready to go up against the Mouse Queen and take her throne, you're going to do who and what I say."

Clara's magic surged up at Konig's commands. She leaned into him as if she liked the way he was being rough with her. Had he worked some dark spell on her?

"Princess, you don't have to do anything he says. You've already got the power of three lands, you can resist him if you want." I yanked on the chains holding me from her even though lightning shot through my broken arm. My pain didn't matter, only hers.

"She'll do what I tell her to, because we both like it when she does." He slid his hand up her throat until the very same thumb he'd sucked on early pressed against her bottom lip. "If I want her to drop to her knees and suck my cock, or yours for that matter, she would. Isn't that right, my queen?"

That telltale flush from her arousal spiked up her throat and cheeks and she nodded, opened her mouth, and licked the tip of his thumb. "I've wanted you both since the first moment I saw you in our great room. I thought it was all a dream then."

She dropped the blankets wrapped around her to the floor, displaying her beautiful body for the two of us. I hated that my cock responded when it was clear that something was wrong. Her magic wasn't just wisps swirling around like when she'd consummated her bond with the others. It literally pulsed like a heartbeat up and down her breasts, stomach, and thighs.

"What have you done to her?"

"This is all her, the real Clara you've been too chaste to see." Konig slid his hand between her thighs, and she arched into him. "I may be giving the commands, but she's the Queen of Spirit and Magic. This is her domain."

Holy Christmas star. She hadn't been drained of her power when we'd come through the rift and into her desolate land, she'd been absorbing the magic and power that remained, and now she was drunk on it. "Clara, love, listen to me. You can't take all this magic in. It's too much, you're not ready."

Her eyes snapped open, and the red magic of her land sparkled in her irises. "You're wrong, nutcracker. Do you think you haven't prepared me? All that I'm missing now is the bond with the land of the Snowflakes and the Land of Animals, and then I can complete my mission."

She walked toward me, slowly, like a seductress come to steal my spirit. This wasn't the Clara I knew and loved.

I swallowed hard past the lump of dread in my throat to ask this question. "To usurp the Mouse Queen?"

"No." She smiled but not in that lovely uncompli-cated way from her first few days here. This smile was the kind I'd seen on Zucker's face a hundred times, when he had sex on the brain. "That's never what I was here to do."

I didn't know what to do with that. Her magic was calling to that fire in my blood, and I was scared to death of this seductive magician she was becoming before my eyes. Since the night we were all born under the Christmas Star, those that fought against the tyrant magicians and later the Mouse Queen, believed the Stahlbaums were free from the taint of power the rest of their ilk. The Queen of Spirit and Magic alone wasn't corrupted and that someday her children would return and together we would bring the Winter Realm back to the peaceful land of the past.

Clara's magic was corrupting her before my eyes, spurred on my Konig's domination of her. He'd already proven he'd chose power, glory, and position over doing what was right. I could do nothing to stop her if she decided she wanted to take over the realm without the rest of us by her side.

Or just the Mouse Prince as her lone consort.

I couldn't let that happen.

I had never known what my role in her magic would be, unlike the others whose gifts were so obvious. It was why I pushed hard to have courage, be a leader, and take on the most dangerous of missions like passing through the veil between our worlds to bring her back to the Winter Realm. While I could access her power, I was no messiah or savior as my people believed.

But perhaps I could be her savior.

Only if I could access her magic, and I couldn't do that chained to the wall. "My lady, I am yours no matter your path. What would you have me do to serve you?"

Konig narrowed his eyes at me but continued to watch Clara's approach. My mouth became the desert and my blood the sun beating down on my spirit with desperate heat.

"I want only what you're unprepared to give me." She pressed her body to mine and for once in my life, I wished my clothes gone and to press my bare chest against hers.

Konig moved close, flanking her from behind. He leaned in and whispered in her ear. "Then take what you want from him, my Queen."

When she looked up into my eyes, they were clear, not clouded with magic. Perhaps I could still reach my Clara. I wasn't good with words like Tau and couldn't charm her like Zucker. But I had to try. I didn't even know what to say. But I would simply speak from my heart and rely on the power and magic of love.

She knew and understood that. Her bondings with the others had let me feel how deep her love ran. It was her life's blood, and that which made her magic so powerful. It was that which made us all believe she was the one who could save us all from the catastrophe we'd wrought upon our own realm.

Before I even had a chance to appeal to her, she grabbed the fabric of my shirt and tore it open, sending the buttons flying. Heat flared in her eyes, and she licked her lips. I shivered as she traced her fingers down my skin and fuck if it didn't feel good. Her touch was all I'd ever dreamed of. A trail of her magic sparkled down the path and spread across my skin. The pain in my arm lessened, although didn't go away completely.

She kept going down my stomach, and unbuckled my pants, tugging them down over my hips. My heart was ready to beat out of my chest and my cock stood tall and erect for her. The cool air of the barren castle ruins was no match for the heat of her body. If I wasn't chained to this wall, I would take her now and happily give up my vow of celibacy. It didn't matter anymore, none of my life as the Prince of Snowflakes meant a damn compared to the magic of being with her.

"He's dying for you to touch him. Can you see how much he wants you?" He grasped her hands in his and guided her fingers toward my cock.

Of course I wanted her, but why was Konig doing this? What was his endgame here?

Clara took a long steadying breath and dropped her hands. "No. Not without the Snowflake crown. Because with it, the sex will be meaningless to Nuss. We've waited what feels like a lifetime to make this connection between our spirits. I won't do it without the bond set in place between us."

Thank the fucking Christmas Star. I knew the real Clara was still in there, I knew it.

Konig nuzzled her ear and caressed her breasts. "Then you'll just have to come back to bed with me."

Her eyes fluttered shut and even behind her eyelids the red magic glowed. It returned to her skin and pulsed through her again. "I want the bond with you too, Prince of Animals. Where is your crown? Shall I use my magic to find them both?"

"Yes," I said.

"No," Konig growled. "The crown of the Land of Animals is buried somewhere so dark and deep, that it can never be recovered."

She spun in his grasp and placed her hand over his heart. The pulsing magic poured from her into him until he stumbled back breaking their connection. For a brief moment, I felt the anger in his spirit, but the love and confusion in hers.

"What are you hiding from us, mouse?" I yanked the chains, wanting so much to break free and stop this madness.

The anger faded from his face and was replaced with a smug smile. "Our luscious Clara's need for you is hotter than I expected. I'm going to have a lot of fun making sure you get to see over second of me fucking her, wearing this."

He reached inside of his shirt and pulled up a chain,

at the end of which, the Snowflake Crown swung back and forth, sparking in the firelight.

DEAR READER~

Princess Clara and her Nutcracker Guards' adventures in the Winter Realm aren't over yet. Their story finishes in book three - Crowned.

ACKNOWLEDGMENTS

Special thanks to my Mushroom Mastermind, M. Guida, JL Madore, Dylann Crush, Bri Blackwood, and Claudia Burgoa, for being great friends who know that believe in me and help me keep calm and carry on, even when I think I've screw up my career or have planned the impossible.

I am so very grateful to have readers who will join my on my crazy book adventures. I know this isn't what I typically write - no dragons, no wolves, no witches... but there will ALWAYS be curvy girls getting happy ever afters!

Without all of you, I wouldn't be able to feed my cats (or live the dream of a creative life!)

Thank you so much to all my Patreon Book Dragons!

An enormous thanks to my Official Biggest Fans Ever. You're the best book dragons a curvy girl author could ask for~

Thank you so much for all your undying devotion

for me and the characters I write. You keep me writing (almost) every day.

Hugs and Kisses and Signed Books and Swag for you from me!

- Helena E.
- Alida H.
- Daphine G.
- Bridget M.
- Stephanie F.

Shout out to my Official VIP Fans!
Extra Hugs to you ~

- Heather R.
- Jeanette M.
- Kerrie M.
- Frania G.
- Michele C.
- Tina C.

Tease Me

Unmask Me

Bite Me

Cage Me

Baby Me

Defy Me

Surprise Me

Dirty Dragon

Crave Me

Slay Me

Fated For Curves

A Touch of Fate

A Tangled Fate

A Twist of Fate

The Curvy Love Series

Curvy Diversion

Curvy Temptation

Curvy Persuasion

The Curvy Seduction Saga

Rebound

Rebellion

Reignite

Rejoice

Revel

ABOUT THE AUTHOR

Aidy Award is a curvy girl who kind of has a thing for stormtroopers. She's also the author of the popular Curvy Love series and the hot new Dragons Love Curves series.

She writes curvy girl erotic romance, about real love, and dirty fun, with happy ever afters because every woman deserves great sex and even better romance, no matter her size, shape, or what the scale says.

Read the delicious tales of hot heroes and curvy heroines come to life under the covers and between the pages of Aidy's books. Then let her know because she really does want to hear from her readers.

Connect with Aidy on her website. www.AidyAward.com get her Curvy Connection, and join her Facebook Group - Aidy's Amazeballs.

Printed in Great Britain
by Amazon